The more of Mac's body that remained covered the better.

Jessie had found it increasingly difficult to keep her mind on landscaping and off how he'd look stripped of his clothes and in *her* oversize tub. She had bubble bath, and more, she'd gladly share.

A bead of sweat dropped into her eye, pulling her out of her fantasy. Oh Lord, she was losing it. Too long in the sun. Too much exposure to a man wrong for her in too many ways to count.

She'd never intended to work on her backyard before the wedding. But she had needed a guaranteed distraction that would keep her too busy to think about, let alone fantasize about, a man completely off-limits.

Boy, had that plan backfired.

Dear Reader,

From hardworking singles to loving sisters, this month's books are filled with lively, engaging heroines offering you an invitation into the world of Silhouette Romance…where fairy tales really do come true!

Arabia comes to America in the sultry, seductive *Engaged to the Sheik* (SR #1750) by Sue Swift, the fourth tale of the spellbinding IN A FAIRY TALE WORLD… miniseries. When a matchmaking princess leads a sexy sheik and a chic city girl into a fake engagement, tempers—and sparks—are sure to fly. Don't miss a moment of the magic!

All work is lots of fun when you're falling for the boss—and his adorable baby girl! Raye Morgan launches her BOARDROOM BRIDES miniseries with *The Boss, the Baby and Me* (SR #1751) in which a working girl discovers the high-powered exec she *thought* was a snake in the grass is actually the man of her dreams.

Twin sisters are supposed to help each other out. So when her glamorous business-minded sister gets cold feet, this staid schoolteacher agrees to switch places—as the bride! Will becoming *The Substitute Fiancée* (SR #1752) lead to happily ever after? Find out in this romantic tale from Rebecca Russell.

Rediscover the miracle of forgiveness in the latest book from DeAnna Talcott, *A Ring and a Rainbow* (SR #1753). As childhood sweethearts they'd promised each other forever, but that was a long time ago. Can these two adults get past their heartbreak to face the reality of a life together?

Sincerely,

Mavis C. Allen
Associate Senior Editor

Please address questions and book requests to:
Silhouette Reader Service
U.S.: 3010 Walden Ave., P.O. Box 1325, Buffalo, NY 14269
Canadian: P.O. Box 609, Fort Erie, Ont. L2A 5X3

The Substitute Fiancée

REBECCA RUSSELL

SILHOUETTE *Romance*®

Published by Silhouette Books

America's Publisher of Contemporary Romance

To Carole. I'm so blessed to have a sister to share childhood
memories with, and I'm looking forward to creating more
wonderful memories with each passing year.

And a big thanks to Vicki, Tammy, Karen, Judy and
Rob for all the brainstorming, critiques and
unwavering support. You're the best!

 SILHOUETTE BOOKS

ISBN 0-373-19752-7

THE SUBSTITUTE FIANCÉE

Copyright © 2005 by Rebecca Russell

This edition published by arrangement with Harlequin Books S.A.

Visit Silhouette Books at www.eHarlequin.com

Printed in U.S.A.

Books by Rebecca Russell

Silhouette Romance

Right Where He Belongs #1575
The Substitute Fiancée #1752

REBECCA RUSSELL

Between racquetball, hockey, volunteering, writing and family, Rebecca Russell is an "at home" mom who is rarely home! She lives with her husband of nineteen years and a teenage son and daughter in Plano, Texas. Although grounded in her suburban life and small-town Ohio roots, Rebecca loves to spend time with flawed but heroic characters who find love and a happy ending.

Rebecca loves to hear from readers. You can write her at P.O. Box 852125, Richardson, TX 75085-2125, or e-mail her at rebecca_russell_22@yahoo.com.

Prologue

"It's bad luck to see your fiancée in her dress before the wedding, Mr. McKenna," advised the woman draped in pearls and armed with a clipboard and pen. She stood dead center in a hallway decorated with wedding portraits of several famous pro football players.

Too bad the skilled but overpaid athletes couldn't hop out of the pictures and run some interference right now, Mac McKenna thought wryly. He settled for a glare instead.

But the petite, obviously stubborn woman blocking his path didn't blink, let alone budge.

"Are you sure I can't convince you to wait out front?" the woman persisted.

Mac shook his head. He had no intention of spending one more minute than necessary in the main room of Brennan's, *the* bridal boutique favored by the upper-crust of Dallas.

He'd never seen so many fussy, frilly things. Designer gowns tucked in clear plastic bags had taken over an entire wall. The satin shoes looked too pristine to wear, the intricate beading on the veils and gloves too delicate to actually use.

"Sir?"

"We're not the superstitious type." Besides, Jenna had asked him to come and give his opinion on the gown. For some reason, Jenna, usually independent and confident, had become a bundle of uncertainty since he'd proposed to her two months ago.

"Very well. Come with me. Ms. Taggert is in the first room."

He followed the woman inside and stopped next to the couch; he wouldn't be around long enough to sit. Jenna, wrapped in a swirl of cream-colored satin and lace, stood on a raised platform in front of a tri-fold mirror.

She looked stunning as always, her makeup perfect, every long blond hair in place. But instead of her trademark sexy smile, a pout marred her beautiful face.

"Are you sure this is the right dress for me, Mac?" She turned around slowly and studied the gown from every angle. "Maybe I should go with the Vera Wang. It has the beadwork I like."

"It's your call, Jenna, but this one looks fine to me."

Jenna tossed her hair back and faced the mirror once again. "Fine? I don't want a dress that's just fine." She sighed. "I'm marrying Dallas's top trial lawyer. I need to impress. I guess I'll just have to go through them all again."

Mac checked his watch and fought a rising impatience. Jenna had given him the impression she had already made her decision and just wanted his approval. She of all people knew how his clients depended on him, how he committed one hundred and ten percent effort toward a win in the courtroom and didn't have time to waste.

He caught the gaze of the consultant. "Can you give us a minute?"

She nodded and disappeared.

He approached his fiancée, who had always personified confidence but now seemed like some confused stranger. "I got to the number one spot because I'm tenacious about going after doctors and hospitals who are negligent." He put his hands on her shoulders. "You have great taste. Just pick a dress, then meet me back at the office. We need to build an airtight case against the dirtbag of a doctor who almost cost the Carrolls their daughter's life."

"You're right." Jenna called for the consultant, who quickly reappeared. "Bring me the other five dresses that I narrowed it down to last week, and can you hurry?"

Jenna kissed his cheek. "You go on, and I'll be there shortly. Promise."

Mac made a quick exit, annoyed over the wasted trip and still perplexed by Jenna's behavior. He had heard that wedding planning could cause stress, but he'd assumed she would handle it with the same confidence and focus she'd shown in her work since her first day of internship four years ago.

Three months earlier, when he'd offered her a partnership with the firm as a reward for such dedication, she'd quickly accepted, then surprised him with an offer of her own. "Why not take the partnership one step further?" she'd boldly suggested.

Both of them were smart, ambitious and competitive. Why not date, see if they were as perfect for each other outside the law firm as well? Where else would he find a woman who wouldn't resent the long hours he devoted to ensuring doctors, hospitals and insurance companies were held accountable when they screwed up? Separately, he and Jenna could do great things, but together, they'd be unstoppable.

Mac couldn't find any holes in her theory. Besides, at thirty-eight he was tired of living alone, but too dedicated to his practice to make the time to meet women outside of work.

So, after several dates he'd ascertained they were compatible on many levels, the most important being that she was just as consumed by her career as he was and had no interest in ever having children. He then did the logical thing and proposed marriage.

But he'd never anticipated that she'd have a meltdown.

Surely after the wedding the old Jenna would reappear. Unless…had he jinxed his marriage by seeing his fiancée in her wedding dress before the ceremony?

He shook his head and chuckled at the uncharacteristically whimsical notion. No way. Jenna was the perfect woman for him; she and the high-priced wedding consultant had all the wedding plans under control and would leave nothing to chance. No silly superstition could compete, let alone win out, over logic.

Chapter One

Jessie Taggert reached into her locker at the health club for her swimsuit, eager to hit the whirlpool after an intense workout. The nearly scalding, bubbling water would feel great on her tired muscles.

An unfamiliar jingle erupted from her gym bag. She frowned in confusion as she retrieved her cell phone, then chuckled at the realization that her twin sister must've changed the ring again, an ongoing joke. Jenna was a true techie, while Jessie, who admittedly enjoyed the convenience of cell phones and computers, worked on a need-to-know basis. "Hello."

"Jessie, thank God I caught you."

Alarms went off in Jessie's head. Her sister sounded frantic. Jenna didn't panic easily. "What's wrong?"

"Everything. Nothing. I mean, I need you to do me a favor."

Jessie groaned. "Come on, Jenna, it's my vacation." She loved her job teaching third grade, but the summers off kept getting shorter every year for both teachers and students. "Can't you get someone else to do whatever it is?"

"Not this time. I got called out of town. I'll be back tomorrow morning, but it means I can't make the final fitting for my wedding dress today. We're the same size and since we're identical, no one will know it's not me."

"But it's only been two months since you bought the dress. Why would you even need another fitting?"

"It's Brennan's policy. Can you be there at noon?"

Jessie glanced at her watch. "You're giving me an hour's notice?"

"Please, Jessie. I really need you to do this for me. My wedding is in seven days. I'd do it for you."

Jessie couldn't argue that point. Two sisters couldn't be more different, but they had always been there for each other. "I thought you were taking this whole week off to do nothing *but* get ready for the wedding."

"I was, I mean, I am, but something important came up. You're a doll for helping me. And one more thing, you absolutely cannot tell Mac or anyone else that I've left town."

"But isn't your trip business related?" Why else would her career-minded twin go out of town right before her wedding to the attractive but equally ambitious attorney?

"I'll explain later. Just promise me."

"Okay, I promise, but—"

"Thanks, sis."

Jessie didn't bother to protest, having learned long

ago that her sister, older by two minutes, usually got what she wanted. Jenna had always possessed a penchant for intrigue, but a week before her wedding?

Jessie hung up and shoved the phone back into her bag, disappointed that she had to trade a relaxing soak and sauna for a quick shower, but at least it was for something worthwhile.

Since her engagement to Mac McKenna, Jenna had been busier than ever, but she seemed happy. She proudly claimed that Mac had finally met his match. He planned to stay on top as a trial lawyer who attracted Dallas's most controversial cases, and her goal was to become every bit as successful.

They had begun the search for a house. No doubt, hired help would do the housekeeping, lawn and pool care so that the busy attorneys' time and energy could be channeled into their careers. Neither wanted children—too much of a distraction.

They were perfect for each other.

Jessie couldn't imagine a more empty existence, but this wasn't about her. After a shower, she'd race the twenty or so miles from Plano to downtown Dallas. She'd take the tollway, the quickest route. Still, she'd be hard-pressed to make the drive to the bridal shop in an hour.

Jenna was going to owe big-time for this favor.

Jessie hurried through the front door of Brennan's Bridal Boutique and her eyes immediately began to burn from the battle of heavy perfumes.

Women of all shapes and sizes decked out in Prada,

Gucci and big hair milled about the room. A few customers even carried pets in designer totes.

Jessie suddenly felt self-conscious in her lightweight jogging suit, ponytail and no makeup, but at least she was clean.

Conversation competed with soft jazz that flowed from hidden speakers as she scanned the room for a glimpse of "the pearl lady," Jenna's description of her bridal consultant.

A petite woman in pearls seemed to appear out of nowhere and appraised Jessie over reading glasses. "Ms. Taggert, I almost didn't recognize you."

The woman's scrutiny left Jessie squirming in her no-brand tennis shoes. "I had something come up at the last minute, so I either had to reschedule or come like this."

"These things happen, I suppose. And since your wedding is next week, you made the right decision. I have a changing room all ready for you, so follow me."

The consultant stepped into a short hallway that boasted thick cream carpet and white walls adorned with wedding portraits of local celebrities. "I double-checked that the fitter made the tucks in the waist just as you requested. I hope it meets with your approval, because we really are running out of time."

Jessie smiled. "I'm sure it'll be fine."

The consultant stopped in front of the first door, gave Jessie a puzzled look, then motioned her inside.

Jessie entered a spacious room furnished with a couch, a huge trifold mirror and a circular raised platform in front of it.

A gown that screamed "Look at me" hung next to a

plush white robe. Nestled below was a pair of off-white satin pumps dyed to match the dress.

Jessie frowned. Whatever happened to simple and elegant?

"Ms. Taggert, is something wrong with the dress?"

Jessie forced a smile. "No. Of course not." Her opinion of the gown didn't matter. "I'll try this on and be out of your hair in no time."

"Wonderful. Here, let me help—"

"Thanks, but I can manage."

After another strange look, and obvious reluctance, the consultant left.

Jessie stepped into the fussy gown. The dress hugged and flared in all the right places, as far as she could tell. She checked the time. With any luck, ten minutes, fifteen tops, she'd be out of there and on her way home to play in her garden.

"Jenna, are you in there? I need to talk to you."

Mac! She'd only met her sister's fiancé once, but his deep, sexy voice was easily recognizable. "I'm sort of busy right now, Mac." What was he doing at a bridal shop? "Later works better for me," she offered. Much later.

"This is important."

Oh, God. Mac didn't sound as if he'd take no for an answer. What was she going to do? "But you can't see me in my dress before the wedding."

"Now I *know* something is wrong." His voice sounded closer. "I saw you in it months ago. What's going on?"

Why couldn't her sister have been a more conventional, superstitious bride-to-be? "But that was before changes were made. I want it to be a surprise."

"Forget about the dress. We need to talk. Now."

An all-too-familiar queasiness erupted in Jessie's sensitive stomach, her body's typical reaction to stress. She had to come up with some reason to keep Mac out. Jenna *never* went anywhere without makeup and every hair in place.

"You've ignored my calls, Jenna. I've been trying to get ahold of you since yesterday when you missed your appointment to take the deposition for the Grant case. I had to send Adam to cover for you."

Panic gave way to worry. Jenna always put work first. Something really must be wrong, but Jessie couldn't ask Mac about it, since she'd promised to keep her sister's absence a secret.

She needed to talk to Jenna, but first she would have to deal with the tenacious lawyer who would know she wasn't his fiancée after one look at her fresh-scrubbed face. "Okay, Mac, but I need to see the consultant first. Will you find her and send her in?"

Silence followed Jessie's request. What would she do if he just barged in? After all, she didn't really know her sister's fiancé, having met him the first and only time at the couples shower she'd hosted several weeks ago at the Green Room.

He had arrived at the popular Deep Ellum restaurant with Jenna on his arm. Every coal-black hair was in place, his manners polished, as he worked the room like a seasoned politician and flashed his winning smile.

Of course, a man that attractive, that perfect, would choose a woman like Jenna.

He'd kept his arm around Jenna's waist or shoulders the entire time, an obvious sign of affection, but Jessie hadn't been won over. Something wasn't quite right about them as a couple, but she couldn't define what it was and that bothered her.

"Don't take too long, Jenna," Mac warned.

The consultant rushed inside and Jessie shut the door. "I need your help."

"Is something wrong with the dress?"

Jessie shook her head. "The dress is great. But I can't let my fiancé see me like this. Do you have any makeup around here that I can use? I'll be glad to pay you."

The woman's knowing smile might as well have been an "I told you so." No self-respecting woman ever left the house not looking her best. "No need for that. Don't worry, I'll be right back."

While waiting for the cosmetics, Jessie arranged her hair into an elegant knot. As kids, the sisters had often traded places to cover for each other when the need arose. While fooling others entertained Jenna, the charades usually left Jessie reaching for the closest bottle of antacid to calm her nervous digestive system.

Now that she was an adult, deception proved even more difficult to stomach.

"She'll just be a minute, Mr. McKenna," the consultant called over her shoulder as she stepped inside and closed the door behind her. "You'd best hurry, Ms. Taggert. He's wearing a hole in the carpet." She held out a small black vinyl bag. "My makeup should work. We have about the same coloring."

Jessie hugged her. "You're an angel. Thanks." She dug through the cosmetics and pulled out concealer, determined to do the best she could, despite being makeup challenged.

"Don't take this wrong, Ms. Taggert, but you're like a different person this afternoon. When you were here a couple of months ago you couldn't make up your mind about which dress you wanted, and today you barely look at it and say it's fine. Are you sure? Because we want you to be happy with the gown."

Jenna, indecisive? Not likely. The woman must have her customers mixed up. "I'm sure about the dress. It was just wedding jitters before."

Jessie made an attempt to apply the mascara, not surprised to find her hand shaking. What if Mac barged inside before she was ready?

The "pearl lady" smiled. "It happens all the time. Here, let me help you. Your hands are shaking so much you're going to make a mess of it."

Jessie gladly let her guardian angel take charge of the impromptu makeover while she worried about the bigger problem of fooling Mac. Surely she could pull off the charade for such a short amount of time.

Minutes later, with her hair and makeup near-perfect, she felt ready to face the man on the other side of the door who had driven across town in search of answers, answers she didn't have to give. After more heartfelt thanks, she sent the consultant outside.

Tomorrow, once her sister returned, life could get

back to normal—calm and predictable—the way Jessie preferred it.

She closed her eyes and pictured in her mind how her sister stood, walked and talked, her facial expressions and gestures. Composed, glamorous, perfect.

Oh, God. She couldn't do this, was crazy to think she could fool anyone, let alone Mac.

But she had to at least try. She took some deep breaths. "Time to begin the show," she whispered, then opened the door.

Mac was already walking toward her, a frown etched on his tanned, handsome face. Tall, muscular and completely male, he looked terribly out of place in such a feminine setting, but not lost. Oh, no. The determined set of his jaw revealed he was a man on a mission and he'd reached his target.

She stepped back and gave him what she hoped was a sexy smile as she held out her hand in a stopping motion. "Don't come any closer, Mac. This dress cost a fortune and I wouldn't want any beads to come loose."

She wanted to give him every reason *not* to touch her. She already felt bad enough about the deception and wanted to limit the contact.

As if he hadn't heard, or simply didn't care, he shut the door behind him and moved toward her until he stood close enough for her to notice flecks of gold in his brown eyes, reminding her of dark chocolate swirled with caramel.

His cologne made her think of fast cars, sure hands and slow, torturous kisses.

"I'll pay for the repairs."

He put his hands on her shoulders. An incredible warmth flooded her body. His intensity, completely focused on her, sucked all the air out of the room.

Her legs grew weak and she teetered on the borrowed high heels.

"Jenna, what's wrong?" Strong hands guided her to the couch several feet in front of the trifold mirror and helped her take a seat. "Are you sick?" he asked as he sat next to her.

"N…no. I'm just frazzled, I guess." *And hating that I've been put into the position of deceiving you.*

He held both her hands and studied her face for what seemed like hours. The innocent contact turned Jessie's limbs more rubbery and useless than spending too long in the hot tub. Thank goodness she was already sitting down.

Why did the man have to be so gorgeous and sexy? Any woman with a breath left in her would have trouble remaining immune to his presence, she reasoned, and her own frantic pulse made it clear she was very much alive.

Jessie cursed her body for reacting to Mac, who wasn't even her type. Bossy workaholics who had no interest in ever becoming a father held no appeal for her.

And besides, a hotshot lawyer such as Mac wouldn't be impressed by a woman who was passionate about teaching, and preferred digging in a garden to attending a fancy party.

None of this even mattered, though. He was her sister's fiancé, enough said.

"You never get frazzled, Jenna."

Jessie thrust out her chin, the way she imagined her sister would. "Well, this is my first wedding. I'm entitled."

"Okay, but that doesn't explain why you missed an appointment yesterday, and didn't return my calls."

Jenna had arranged to have the following week off to focus on wedding plans; she would never start her vacation early without clearing it first. What was she up to? "Look, Mac, I'm sorry I let the firm down. It won't happen again. I just needed some time to myself so I turned off all the phones. This whole wedding thing is making me a little crazy."

"But why? You hired the best wedding planner in Dallas, all the choices have been made. And you're already taking off next week to finalize the wedding plans."

She sensed his patience was wearing thin. "I can't explain it, Mac. Just accept that I'll probably keep a low profile until this is all over, and that I might not be myself."

"Since your desk is cleared, I don't see a problem if you want to start lying low on Monday."

Alarms sounded in her head once again. "I'm thinking I'd rather start now."

He frowned. "Are you sure you're all right?"

"Yes. Why?"

"It's not like you to forget, let alone pass up, a photo op like the C.D.R. fund-raiser tonight or dinner with your family tomorrow."

Jessie quickly dismissed the obligatory meal with her parents as a problem. Her sister would be back by then. But how could Jenna, who lived for the spotlight, have forgotten the Childhood Disease Research bash, the society event of the year? And it was tonight!

She'd get Jenna on the phone, remind her of the fund-raiser and insist she return home. Immediately.

Jessie forced a smile as her mind raced to find a believable explanation for "her" memory lapse. Of course he'd be surprised if her sister had forgotten an opportunity to rub elbows with the rich and famous, people she hoped would soon end up on her client list. "I guess I'm more frazzled than I realized, Mac. I completely forgot about the party tonight, and I just assumed you knew skipping the Sunday family dinner wasn't an option."

"I've never seen this side of you before."

"Weddings will do that to a girl."

"Are you sorry you let me off the hook and said you'd plan the wedding so that I could keep working up to the last minute, that all I had to do was show up?"

Jessie didn't know which made her more sad, the fact he had zero interest in planning his own wedding, or that her sister preferred it that way. "No, not at all. You'd just be in the way."

He smiled, but seemed distracted. "Now you're sounding like the old Jenna. You were right. We do make a great team, and part of it is because you're just as driven as I am."

Jessie would never comprehend work being a person's only priority, but guessed she didn't have to. Jenna put her career first, as did Mac, and that was obviously the life they wanted. If her sister was happy, nothing else mattered.

He glanced at his watch and stood. "I need to get back to the office. I'll pick you up at eight."

Oh, Lord. The fund-raiser. If Jenna followed her recent pattern of not returning calls when it proved convenient, Jessie would have no choice but to continue the charade into the evening.

Her sister would know the appropriate attire for the gala, but Jessie had no clue. "What suit are you wearing? I don't want to clash."

"My Armani. Dark blue," he said, then absently brushed his lips across her cheek, his mind obviously already focused on the work waiting for him. He opened the door, then disappeared into the hallway.

As Jessie closed the door, she fought back the urge to call after him and ask if he planned to work on his wedding day and during the honeymoon, then quickly reminded herself it wasn't any of her business.

Besides, she had bigger, more immediate issues to worry about. The party was only seven hours away.

"Will you be taking the dress with you?" the consultant asked through the door. "Or do you want it sent to your apartment?"

"Send it, please." Jessie had enough to deal with right now. With great care she hurried out of the dress, then grabbed the phone from her purse and called Jenna. Voice mail. Not a good sign.

Jessie left an urgent message for Jenna to call back immediately, along with a reminder about the fundraiser that evening.

"Is there anything else I can do for you, Ms. Taggert?"

"Not unless this store sells fairy godmothers," Jessie mumbled as she threw on her own clothes. She wasn't a pessimist by nature, but she couldn't summon much hope that her sister would call, let alone return home in time to attend the fund-raiser.

She never should have promised to keep her sister's absence a secret.

"Did you say something, ma'am?"

"No. I'm all set. Thanks."

All set for disaster, Jessie silently added, if her sister remained out of touch and out of town.

Jessie had to prepare for the worst, which meant that in the next seven hours she needed to come up with a plan for how to transform "Plain Jane" Jessie into "Glamour Gal" Jenna.

Chapter Two

"I have a bad feeling about tonight." Jessie took a seat on the small bench in front of her sister's bathroom mirror. Her two closest friends, Carla and Dana, stood on either side of her.

"Think positive thoughts," Carla replied. "And quit frowning. You'll get wrinkles."

Jessie reached for the can of soda in front of her, struggled to flick the tab, but soon gave up rather than risk ruining her newly painted nails.

She stared at her hands and the French manicure. Tips had been added to her own nails to make her even more identical to her mysteriously absent sister. Already she was beginning to feel like someone else and she didn't like it one bit.

Dana reached for the soda, opened it and gave the can back to Jessie.

"Thanks, Dana." Jessie took a drink and hoped the carbonated beverage would calm her stomach. "How does Jenna, or anyone for that matter, function with nails this long? I can't even open a soda with these things."

Carla shook her head and sighed. "Jessie, hon, you're missing the whole point about the advantages of being a glamorous woman." Petite, curvy and beautiful with big blond hair, Carla had "former Dallas debutante" written all over her.

She was also self-deprecating and generous to a fault, which made her a great neighbor and an even better friend. "Men will fall over backward to do whatever you need done, whether it's opening a can or a door. But glamour is as much about attitude as it is looks."

"And I'm sure you'll get used to the nails," offered Dana, a fellow teacher and terrible liar.

"In two hours? I doubt it. Since Jenna has refused to return my calls, it would serve her right if I just told Mac the truth."

"It would, but you won't," Carla chided. "You made a promise and besides, she's your sister and family sticks together."

"Sister or not, once I know she's okay I'm going to strangle her for putting me in this position." Jessie pulled her friends close. "Thank heavens you're both here. I wouldn't have a chance of pulling this off without your help."

Carla had called in favors to get a last-minute nail appointment and Dana, who had put herself through college working as a hair stylist, had tugged and poked Jessie's hair into an elegant updo.

They had driven in separate cars to Jenna's downtown loft apartment, since they needed access to her makeup and clothes and that's where Mac would pick Jessie up for the party.

The entire time, Jessie had kept her cell phone on and within sight, praying that she'd get the call saying Jenna was back in town and ready to jump back into her life.

"Trust me, this is more fun than doing laundry, my usual Saturday plans." Dana peered into a basket on the counter filled with sample-size soaps and lotions. "Hey, isn't that Jenna's engagement ring?"

Carla reached for the ring and held it up for all to see. The huge, clear diamond sparkled under the lights. "Sure is. But why would she leave it behind?"

Dana's eyes grew wide. "She wouldn't, unless she knew all along she wouldn't be back in time for tonight. Jessie would need it to pull off the switch."

Jessie's stomach protested at the possibility that her sister had planned to be gone for the fitting and the party. That she'd set up her twin to be a part of such an uncomfortable deception.

"According to Mac, Jenna's been acting strange all week, but she hasn't mentioned anything to me." Jessie wished she knew if her sister was just experiencing a severe case of cold feet or if she was in real trouble, or something else entirely.

Carla frowned. "Don't twins have a special connection, you know, where you sense what the other one is thinking or feeling?"

Jessie nodded. "I've experienced some of that, but it's not so simple." When they were younger, she had competed against Jenna for their parents' attention. As teen-agers, their desire to be seen as individuals had kept her and Jenna from being super close, like many twins. "I think I'd know if she was in real danger," Jessie added, "but all I got from her last phone call was that she was under a lot of pressure."

"It probably doesn't help that you're both so differ-ent. You'd never go for a rock like this for an engage-ment ring. Your house is so warm and cozy, and while this place is beautiful…" Carla's voice trailed off as she studied the funky chrome light fixtures suspended from the ceiling. "It's a little—"

Dana leaned against the green marble vanity. "Cold and pretentious?"

"Not at all," Carla protested. "I was going to say modern."

"Stay focused ladies," Jessie pleaded. "It's because my sister and I are so different that I'm in a panic."

"Jessie, hon, I don't want to add to your worries, but have you thought about what happens tonight *after* the fund-raiser? Let's face it, you and Jenna are completely different when it comes to relationships, too. You like to play it safe and take your time get-ting to know someone and she's more, well, adven-turous. Not that there's anything wrong with that, but she and Mac are probably sleeping together, don't you think?"

An all too familiar queasiness crept up on Jessie and she clutched her stomach. She'd been stressing over minor things like nails and makeup, when a much bigger problem existed. "Oh, God. You're right. I mean, she's never talked about it, which is strange for her, but still, odds are you're right. What am I going to do?"

Dana patted Jessie's shoulder. "With your nervous stomach, by the end of the night you'll probably really be sick and then you won't have to act."

Jessie groaned at the prospect and hoped she had plenty of antacids in her purse.

"I know it looks like Jenna has set you up and lied," Carla said. "But you're the one who's always telling me to keep an open mind until I have all the facts."

Carla gently cupped Jessie's chin and turned it until she faced the mirror. "Jessie, as crazy as Jenna makes you sometimes, she's your sister and is depending on you. You can do this. You'll just be playing pretend for a couple of hours and I doubt you'll have to worry about opening cans of soda at a posh fund-raiser. And you can take your pick of excuses—a headache, cramps, upset stomach. Unless he's a jerk, he won't press spending the night, right?"

Jessie forced a smile and cursed the fact that her friend knew how much family meant to her. "Right."

"That's my girl." Carla grinned. "Now, put on the ring before you forget."

Whatever her sister's reasons for leaving behind her engagement ring, Jessie had no choice. As she eased the three-carat ring onto her finger, uneasiness and panic raced up and down her spine. No prior deception, no prank had ever felt so wrong.

Still, Jessie couldn't let her sister down.

"I'll help you with the makeup, Jess. Dana, you

choose an outfit, something dressy, but not too flashy. And try to find one that's tea length so she doesn't have to worry about hose."

Dana saluted and hurried into the walk-in closet. "Wow," she called out. "I feel like I'm in designer-label heaven."

Carla rubbed her hands together, her expression gleeful as she surveyed a drawer crammed full of every cosmetic imaginable. "Trust me, Jessie, you're going to knock Mac off his feet."

Jessie believed her friends had the skill to make her look the part, but she had tons of doubt regarding her ability to pull off the act if, as Carla claimed, being glamorous required attitude more than anything else.

On the positive side, the awkwardness of her new nails now seemed a minor problem compared to the concern over her sister's absence, Jessie's guilt for deceiving Mac and the worry of how she was going to keep him out of her bed at the end of the evening.

Mac fought a sense of foreboding as he rang the doorbell to Jenna's apartment. Who would he find tonight? The confident, bold Jenna of old or the new, uncertain, vulnerable Jenna of late?

He disliked disruption in his routine and was still on edge from this morning when, for the first time ever, he'd found it difficult to concentrate on his work after he'd returned from the bridal shop.

His mind had continually drifted back to his reaction to Jenna's confession to feeling overwhelmed by wedding plans. An immediate protectiveness had surfaced out of nowhere, unnerving him to the point he'd made the quickest possible exit from the store.

Unfortunately, all he'd managed to accomplish that afternoon was rearranging the piles on his desk and reading the same brief three times without one word penetrating his unfocused brain.

He heard a clinking noise, a muffled curse, then the door opened. Jenna's one hand gripped the tips of the fingers of her other hand, but at least she was dressed and looking her usual glamorous self. Relief ate away at some of his uneasiness.

"You look amazing, as always, Jenna," he said as he drew her close and kissed her on the cheek.

She pulled back and chuckled. "I have to, or everyone will be looking at you!"

"Not a chance with you in the room."

Mac swore he detected a slight flush on Jenna's cheeks, but discarded the idea since she didn't embarrass easily. Must've been the lighting.

"It's settled then, Mac. We're both gorgeous!"

Her smile seemed forced. She reached for her evening bag on the end table and held it against her stomach as if the minuscule purse were a protective shield. But what or who was she guarding herself against?

Jenna wasn't afraid of anyone and was certainly no blushing innocent, so he blamed his vivid imagination tonight on either the lighting or exhaustion.

"Ready?" she asked.

"I was born ready, Jenn," he replied in typical fashion, already anticipating one of her glib comebacks.

Instead, an unmistakable rush of color spread across

her face and he could no longer deny something was different about Jenna today. Their usual banter had never caused a reaction before, not even the times they attempted to outdo each other with sexy double entendres.

Was her odd behavior a result of her having second thoughts about getting married?

He gave himself a mental shake. Jenna was the type of woman who knew what she wanted and went after it, a trait he admired. She'd be the last person to question her decision.

"Let's go then," Jenna finally replied. "We don't want to keep the cameras waiting."

The right words poured from her mouth, but they somehow sounded awkward and her smile seemed too bright. What had happened to her sassy attitude and poise?

She was doing it again, showing a vulnerability he'd never imagined she possessed. What the heck was he supposed to do with vulnerable?

He suddenly knew what he'd like to do. Skip the fund-raiser he'd been in charge of just so he could spend the night kissing the forced smile from her mouth, muss her perfect hair and help her out of the body-hugging pale green dress that matched her eyes.

What was he thinking? No woman, not even his fiancée, had ever tempted him to put pleasure before business.

With a mental shake, he offered his arm. "Let's go," he said more gruffly than intended, but dammit anyway, he'd proposed a merger of talents when he'd asked her to marry him, not an emotional relationship that would distract him from his work.

He'd tolerate her odd behavior for now, but it was countdown time. One week. Just seven more days and his world, and Jenna, had better return to business as usual.

Mac struggled to control his frustration as he searched the crowded ballroom for a sign of Jenna. Not that he'd expected her to remain glued to his side, but she'd been acting so odd lately, he really wanted to keep an eye on her.

He was in his element, so why couldn't he relax? Attendance had doubled in the past three years since he'd become the sponsor of the annual Childhood Disease Research fund-raiser and moved the gala to the Congress Hotel, one of the oldest and finest in downtown Dallas.

He'd obviously chosen the right people for the decorating committee. The ballroom decorations met his standards of simple yet elegant, and the food appeared to be a hit as well. The band, set up in a rear corner, played just loud enough to be heard and not discourage conversation.

Reps from several local TV stations and the newspaper had arrived as promised with camera crews, so the event would get great coverage in both medias.

Where was Jenna?

"You sure know how to throw a party, McKenna."

He turned to discover John Nashco. The district attorney had a reputation as a notorious, but harmless, flirt. "Anything for a good cause. Filled out that check yet?"

John nodded. "But I'd rather let your fiancée sweet-talk me out of it. Won't hurt so much. Where is the captivating Jenna?"

Mac wasn't about to admit he'd been wondering that himself. "You know her, she's working the room." He caught a glimpse of light green fabric. "I see her, John. Stay here and get your checkbook out. I'll be right back."

Mac made his way through the crowd toward Jenna. The closer he got, the more his senses came alive. Her tentative smile charmed, her feminine curves captivated. He was surprised by the warmth in her voice as she spoke to an elderly man he recognized but couldn't place. She usually "worked" a crowd and rarely stopped for a lengthy one-on-one chat.

He put his arm around her shoulders. She immediately stiffened, looked up and smiled, then relaxed against him, their bodies a perfect fit.

Her soft hair tickled his chin and the subtle floral scent kicked his hormones into high gear. Had she recently changed shampoos or had he just somehow failed to notice before? "I need to steal you away for a minute, Jenn."

"Sure." She turned to the man she'd been conversing with. "Tell your wife I hope she feels better soon, Mr. Boreman."

"I will, young lady." He nodded at Mac. "Mr. McKenna, you're a lucky man. Take care of her, you hear?"

"I intend to, sir." Mac took Jenna by the elbow and weaved through the throng of dark suits and sequins. "John Nashco wants to arm wrestle you for a donation."

"Arm wrestle? You're kidding, right?"

Mac raised his eyebrows. "Of course. Just charm the check out of him like you usually do."

"Um, sure. No problem." She glanced around the room, as if looking for an escape. Or had his imagination kicked in again and she was just thirsty and simply looking for a waiter?

"Can I get you anything to drink or eat?"

"I couldn't eat, but a soda would be great."

"A soda?"

She nodded and placed her hands over her stomach. "My stomach is a little unsettled, so I'm going to pass on the wine."

"There you are, Jenna." John kissed her first on one cheek then the other. Her green eyes grew wide for just a second. "You look ravishing, as always."

Those same eyes now sparkled with delight as she curtsied. "Why, thank you, kind sir. And you look rather dashing yourself." She reached for his tie and straightened it. "Great tie."

Mac clenched his jaw to keep from saying anything, then left to find a soda for Jenna instead of her usual Chablis. He needed something stronger for himself before he acted like a fool and wedged his body between theirs.

What was wrong with him? Jenna was just doing what she'd done many times before, stroking a man's ego. Mac trusted her and had never felt the least bit jealous before.

Him, jealous? No. Not possible. They didn't have that kind of a relationship. More than likely, Jenna's weird reaction to the stress of the upcoming nuptials had rubbed off on him.

"How about a couple of pictures, Mr. Nashco, of you and Ms. Taggert?"

Jessie turned to find a young man wearing a media badge and carrying a camera. Her sister lived for these moments in the spotlight, so Jessie put all thoughts of the uncomfortable push-up bra and high heels out of her mind and smiled.

"Any excuse to put my arm around a beautiful lady."

Jessie had to admit that she really did feel beautiful tonight. Before Mac had arrived at the apartment, she'd practiced walking in the high heels as she silently chanted, "Look at me! I'm glamorous. I'm sexy," hoping she could at least fake it until she made it back home.

Of course, the sexy dress and a few drops of her sister's expensive perfume helped to boost her confidence as well.

When she'd opened the door for Mac and observed the approval reflected in his gaze, she'd been relieved. But somehow Jessie had expected more. After all, men who were complete strangers lusted after Jenna, but Jessie didn't detect any such blatant desire in her sister's fiancé.

She just wished she didn't find *him* so darned attractive. She hadn't been exaggerating when she'd claimed just as many eyes would be on him as her tonight. The navy suit, along with his black hair, dark eyes and tanned face proved a striking combination.

His sexy banter had flustered her even more and she was surprised she had to keep reminding herself that he was flirting with his fiancée, not her. Since he wasn't her type, she never dreamed that detail would prove so hard to remember, any more than she would've imagined that his constant, innocent touching would make her feel protected and cherished instead of controlled or possessed.

Then again, tonight she seemed like a stranger even to herself.

"Thanks for the pics. I'll send you both copies."

"Thank *you,* young man." John gave Jessie's shoulder a squeeze. "Jenna, honey, tell me the truth. Why do you want to tie yourself down to a man like Mac when I'm available?"

The guy seemed harmless enough, but she wasn't used to being "on" for so many people and for so long. "John, I know you and Mac are friends so I'm going to pretend I didn't hear that. It's time to give it up. How much are you going to contribute this year to this extremely worthwhile cause?"

John pulled out a folded check from his pants pocket and handed it to her. "Will this suffice?"

She noted the generous amount and kissed him on both cheeks. "My hero. Thank you."

"You're more than welcome. Say, since Mac seems to have deserted us, why don't we—"

"Oh, Mr. Nashco," an elderly woman dripping in diamonds called out as she approached him. "You simply must come meet my darling niece Gracie." She turned to Jessie. "You don't mind, do you, dear?"

"Of course not." Jessie nudged him toward the determined woman. "And thanks again for the donation, John."

The woman practically dragged him off, giving Jessie a much-needed respite from the entertaining but exhausting banter with the infamous prosecutor.

Where had Mac disappeared to? She scanned the crowd for a sign of him, but only because he supposedly had fetched a drink for her, not because she wanted to spend time with him. The more they were together, the higher the risk she'd slip up and reveal her true identity.

In search of something cold to drink, and a diversion, she approached a group of kids hovering around the linen-covered tables laden with exotic finger foods and sparkling bowls of punch.

She poured a cup of the pink liquid for herself and took a long drink. "Hey kids, why the long faces?"

One tall, older boy shrugged, another mumbled under his breath.

The young guests seemed more pale and thin than normal, but what really stood out was their complete boredom.

"I thought this was going to be a *real* party," a young girl with big brown eyes offered.

"Yeah," the mumbler added. "This is lame. I'd rather be back at the hospital playing video games with my buddy."

The tall boy elbowed the "mumbler." "Did y'all forget it was our idea to come tonight?" The spokesman for the group turned to Jessie. "We get so tired of not being able to *do* anything to help. Lots of our friends can't leave the hospital, but we're in remission, so we talked our parents into bringing us with them tonight. They had to fill out all sorts of papers so we could and now it looks like it was all for nothing."

She didn't doubt their sincerity but was still confused. "It's wonderful that you want to help. What was your plan?"

The tall boy shrugged. "We figured if we talked to some of the guests about how we got sick and what we need to get better, that people might understand and give even more. But it's harder to go up and talk to strangers than we thought."

Jessie's heart went out to the brave young souls who had obviously been through more than most kids their age, and to their parents. How did a mother or a father deal with watching their loved one suffer daily as well as live with the fear of losing their child at any moment?

She wanted to do more to help than make a monetary donation, but what? "These people do care or they wouldn't be here tonight," she offered. "And I think they'd love the chance to talk with you, but they have no idea that's why you're here, so we need to get their attention somehow."

She glanced about the room for ideas. At the end of each table sat a balloon bouquet made up of one Mylar balloon and half a dozen of the latex. "Come on, kids. Follow me."

She untied one bouquet and, carrying it like the Olympic torch, headed for an empty corner of the ballroom.

All but the two older boys followed, no doubt too cool for any activity that involved balloons. The rest of the kids, three boys and seven girls ranging from ages six to twelve, she guessed, gazed at her expectantly. "Have you ever done balloon relays?"

All shook their heads.

"Pick a partner, face each other, and form two lines."

As they positioned themselves, she freed two of the latex balloons from the bunch and tied up the ribbon streamers so no one would trip. "Now, the object of the game is to carry the balloon between you and your partner's bellies to the wall and back to the beginning of your line. You can't use your hands. Got it?"

Heads bobbed up and down. Wide eyes sparkled with excitement. Faces beamed.

Jessie helped the first four get into position and then gave the signal to begin.

The kids clapped and cheered for each other as teammates squished the balloons between their bodies and tried to move forward. The balloons fell and were retrieved and repositioned many times. Both groups made it back to the line about the same time and the next four kids took off.

Jessie observed the little brown-eyed girl glancing at one of the older boys. When she failed to get his attention, she hurried over and raised her arms. He shook his head and grinned, then scooped her up and headed over to the game, with the other boy following.

"Squirt here wants me to help her, says she can't go fast enough by herself. Is that okay with you?"

"Of course," Jessie replied. "And your friend here can help, too."

The "mumbler" picked up a small boy and waited for their turn.

To keep the game moving, Jessie helped retrieve the dropped balloons and repositioned them between the bellies. Within minutes, her high heels morphed into torture chambers. Another balloon escaped, but her feet protested the idea of one more chase.

Forget glamour. The kids were having too much fun. The shoes had to go, she decided, and kicked them off. The carpet felt like a caress against her aching bare feet; her toes wiggled with delight at their newfound freedom. Why hadn't she done that earlier?

As the relays continued, Jessie noted the grins that covered the kids' faces. Whether or not her idea worked to draw attention to the children, at least for a little while they had forgotten their reality of doctors, hospitals and treatments.

A hand gripped her elbow, leaving every nerve ending exposed and screaming for more than an innocent touch. Only Mac had that effect on her, much to her surprise and dismay, and she had nowhere to hide.

She was busted.

"What's going on, Jenna?"

Chapter Three

Jessie turned to face Mac and found his gaze puzzled, his frown pronounced. "Why? Is there a problem?" she asked brazenly while her mind raced for a believable explanation for "her" behavior.

How could she have let her guard down even for a minute? Jenna would never have interacted with kids on her own, let alone be caught in bare feet while dressed to the nines.

"This is a fine hotel, not a playground, and kids usually don't even register on your radar."

Jessie stalled for time as she tucked in the strands of hair that had escaped during the numerous balloon retrievals. A quick glance around the room revealed that she had become the center of attention.

Oh, God. She smothered the urge to clench her stomach, which felt as if a medicine ball relay was going on inside of it. She had to respond to him, but hated to lie. She decided to stay as close to the truth as possible. "I know, but some of the kids said the party was lame, and you know how I feel about whiners. So I decided to make them part of the solution to their problem in a way that might help with the fund-raiser."

"Help how?"

"Some of the older kids sounded as if they'd be willing to talk to the guests, put a personal spin on why money is needed. I figured we'd get everyone's attention first, then hand over the microphone to the kids."

"It never occurred to you to run this by me first?"

"Why?" Jessie asked, confident Jenna would never have stopped to ask permission. "It was a win-win situation."

"Jenna, I couldn't help but overhear what you were saying," interrupted an older, distinguished-looking man who had introduced himself earlier as chairman of the board of C.D.R.

"You're a marketing genius," he continued. "I'm going to make a special announcement right now. Keep the kids playing."

The excited chairman, no doubt picturing extra zeroes on checks, hurried off in the direction of the podium.

Unfortunately, Mac still appeared unconvinced. "How did you come up with the game with the balloons?"

"My sister teaches third grade, remember? She mentioned doing balloon relays at one of her homeroom parties and went on ad nauseam about how much the kids loved it. So, I thought, why not give it a shot?"

Seconds ticked by while he mulled over her explanation. Finally, he nodded. "Then I guess you owe your sister a big thank-you for the idea."

Relief calmed Jessie's raging stomach like a fast-acting antacid. "I won't forget, believe me." Only, before the family dinner tomorrow, Jenna would find herself on the receiving end of a tongue thrashing, not a thank-you, for the mess she'd created. "I'm glad you're here now, though. I can use some help chasing after the balloons."

Mac's face turned pale and he backed away as if he'd just been told she were ill and contagious. "Can't. I mean, there are still some people I need to talk to. I'll check back with you later."

Jessie watched Mac disappear into the crowd and wondered if the over-six-foot-tall hunk of a man was afraid of sick kids, then quickly dismissed the notion. If that were true, what reason would he have for being so involved with a research group that focused solely on cures for children?

Another explanation for his odd behavior came to mind but it seemed just as unlikely—Mac was afraid of kids in general.

Mac's hands stung from all the clapping over the past half hour as one by one the children had claimed the floor. In their own honest, unscripted words they conveyed their gratitude for past donations and how crucial research was in order to find cures for childhood diseases.

He was now more determined than ever to continue raising money for research while he worked to gain some sort of justice in the courtroom; unlike these well-treated kids, his clients had suffered at the hands of someone either negligent or without scruples in the medical or insurance profession and deserved compensation.

Mac glanced at Jenna. She appeared as proud and humbled by the strength of the young heroes as he was, and a person would have to be made of stone not to react to the testimonials. Still, he was surprised she'd made no attempt to hide her emotions or tears. Why was he only now seeing this vulnerable side of her? Had she kept any softness hidden, afraid he'd see it as a weakness?

Or was she simply like the other women he'd known in the past who had claimed to be career-driven with no interest in having a family, only to later confess the opposite?

He had thought he'd closed that loophole by proposing to a woman he respected, but did not love. A woman who never claimed to love him, either, but shared his goals.

Had he been played for a fool, again?

The chairman offered his appreciation for everyone's generosity and encouraged all to eat up and drink up while the band played its last set of the evening.

Jenna excused herself and headed in the direction of the children who were being collected by their parents.

Two men cornered Mac with questions about how the research funds were allocated, but he managed to keep an eye on Jenna as she busied herself collecting the balloon bouquets lucky enough to escape the relays. Again, she seemed skittish and in search of an exit.

He accepted checks from the two men, obviously satisfied by his answers, thanked them and shook hands.

His job done for the night, all he wanted to do now was get Jenna alone and find out the answer to *his* question—had she lied to him about not wanting children?

He made his way toward her, but C.D.R.'s chairman of the board reached her first.

"Jenna, my dear, don't bother yourself with cleaning up."

"The staff will deal with that," Mac added, surprised to find Jenna fussing over decorations. Then again, he'd never expected to find her barefoot and playing with a bunch of kids, either.

"I know, but why trash them when you could give the balloons to the hospital? I mean, it would be great PR."

Now *that* sounded like the sharp, image conscious Jenna he knew and wanted as a partner in his law firm.

"That's a wonderful idea. I'll take them by on my way home." The chairman turned to Mac. "Next year, you should make sure Jenna is on the fund-raising committee. She obviously has a feel for this kind of thing."

No way. Tonight had proven Jenna had a soft spot for kids and could be distracted. He'd made her a partner to increase his firm's workload, not deplete it. "Now that she's a partner at the firm, she'll have a full schedule," Mac replied before Jenna could respond. "But I'll be sure and get her input."

"Good enough, Mac. Well, congratulations on another successful gala. We can't thank you enough for all you do for C.D.R."

"It's a great cause." Mac glanced at his watch. "It's late and we need to get going. Good night, sir." He shook hands with the chairman, rushed Jenna's goodbyes to the elderly gentleman, then took her by the elbow and made a quick exit from the ballroom.

Jessie had difficulty keeping up with Mac in her high heels. With every step her anger grew over his blatant display of bad manners, but she refused to sink to his level by making a scene in public.

Once they were out of sight and earshot of those remaining in the ballroom, Jessie came to a complete stop in the hallway that led to the main exit of the hotel. "What was that all about, Mac?"

"What do you mean?"

"Don't play dumb, it doesn't suit you. I'm not taking one more step until you explain why you were so ridiculously rude just now."

He raised an eyebrow. "Are we having our first fight? Here, in a public place?"

"No one is around, and besides, it won't be our last fight if you're going to keep trying to make decisions for me." Jessie knew her sister would never allow Mac or any man to speak for her; she had to fight too hard to be taken seriously, let alone be treated as an equal in a predominantly male profession. Half the time Jenna was mistaken for the court reporter, since some people had trouble believing a lawyer could be blond, built and female.

"You were talking around me as if I wasn't even there. Maybe I'd love to be on the committee next year."

"I thought I was doing you a favor, unless there's more to this than you let on."

Jessie's head spun, unable to even guess where he was going with his innuendo. "You've lost me."

"Can we at least wait to have this discussion in the car?"

"Fine, just so you understand that I'm not letting this go." Jenna for darned sure wouldn't.

When they reached the exit Mac held open the door and they stepped outside into the warm, humid air. He handed the claims ticket to the valet and within minutes his black Porsche appeared.

Fast car. She'd guessed at least one thing right about him based on the cologne he wore. But did he also have sure hands, did he give slow, torturous kisses?

She smothered a groan. What was wrong with her? A scent, no matter how sexy, had never distracted her before, and especially not in the middle of a fight. "What were you implying earlier?" she asked once he had pulled out onto the street, determined to regain her focus. She didn't have much time since her sister lived just a few blocks from the hotel.

Mac cranked up the air-conditioning, which quickly cooled the small enclosed space, but if he had hoped it would chase away her annoyance as well, he was out of luck.

"You seemed pretty at ease with the kids," he replied. "And I'm not buying that it was all a marketing strategy. You were enjoying yourself. Admit it."

She turned sideways in the compact leather seat in an effort to observe his expressions and body language, but the night proved too dark, the streetlights too dim. "What if I was?"

"Then I have to wonder if you've been completely honest with me about not wanting kids of your own."

"Have you changed *your* mind?"

"No. And I won't."

She had to respond, but she wouldn't lie. "Well, I know what I want now, but I certainly can't predict how I'll feel two, three years down the road. No one can."

"I beg to differ. I have my reasons for not wanting a family. The reasons aren't going to change over time, and the why isn't important. Just know that the subject of children is nonnegotiable, Jenna. Be sure that's what you want, too, or it's pointless to go through with the wedding."

Stunned by his fervor and worried she'd screwed up her sister's chance for happiness, all Jessie could think about was escape. Thankfully, the apartment building came into view. "Just drop me off, please."

"I'm walking you to your door." He stopped the car.

"You don't make my decisions for me, remember?" She exited the car, hurried inside the building and into her temporary abode, the sound of his tires squealing against the asphalt still ringing in her ears.

She locked the door behind her, leaned against it and thought how Mac was a lot like the solid, unyielding surface. He was rigid about his priorities; with him, work would always come before a relationship and he did *not* want to be a father. Why? What was he hiding?

And yet, that same man was someone you could depend on; he'd justly earned a reputation as a lawyer you'd want on your side.

Jessie's head hurt from trying to figure him out; her stomach was in knots over the stressful day that had ended in a fight, but at least she no longer had to worry about how she was going to keep him out of her bed….

* * *

Jessie sat at the kitchen table Sunday morning with the thick newspaper and cup of coffee in front of her, but exhaustion wouldn't allow her to appreciate either one.

Concern for her missing sister, who still hadn't called, and worry over her fight with Mac had left Jessie tossing and turning all night. What if she'd caused irreparable damage to her sister's relationship with Mac?

Finally, at eight o'clock, she'd given up on sleep, climbed out of bed and showered. Still no word from her sister.

Jessie took a sip of coffee, found it cold once again and put the mug in the microwave to warm it up.

The timer dinged as the phone rang.

Jessie rushed to the phone. "Hello."

"Hey, sis."

"Jenna, are you okay?"

"I'm all right, I guess."

"Then why aren't you answering your cell? I've been worried sick."

"I know, and I'm sorry. I just couldn't deal with the questions I knew you'd have. I was just too confused."

Jessie sank into the kitchen chair, her body limp with relief. "Confused about what?"

Silence. Not good.

"Jenna, I filled in for you at the dress fitting, which got pretty hairy because Mac showed up. Then I covered your butt at the fund-raiser you somehow forgot to mention. And I've been up all night worried sick because you haven't returned any of my calls. The very least you owe me is an explanation."

"I'm with Dylan."

Jessie sat up straight, her exhaustion forgotten. "You can't be. You're an engaged woman, Jenna."

Jenna sighed. "I knew you wouldn't understand. That's why I couldn't tell you the reason why I left town."

"What's to understand? Engaged women don't leave their engagement ring at home when they leave town or hang out with some drummer they dumped years ago."

"Listen, sis, even *I'm* surprised by how getting married is affecting me. I'm used to running the show, but my emotions seem to be running me since I put that ring on my finger. So, I left the ring behind because I wanted to escape the craziness of the wedding for a while."

Jessie heard the panic and confusion in her sister's voice and wanted to offer reassurance, but she needed more details. She decided to start with what she *did* know. "You broke up with Dylan because you couldn't see a future with him. Has his band suddenly made it big?"

"Only in his dreams. But Thursday night I ran into him at a club where his band was playing. We had a few drinks afterward, just for old time's sake, and the first words out of his mouth were that he should've never let me go. The band was leaving that night for their next gig in Austin and when Dylan asked me to ride along, I said okay."

"Jenna, what were you thinking?"

"I wasn't. That's the problem. The chemistry between us was always incredible and it still is."

"But surely he backed off when you told him you were engaged."

"I, uh, haven't told him, yet."

"What?" Jessie stood and paced, the painted cement floor cool on her bare feet. "You're getting married in a week. That isn't something that just slips your mind."

"Dylan is a stand-up guy. He would've wished me well and sent me on my way, and I had to be sure."

"Now *I'm* confused. Sure of what?"

"Sure that I can live without fireworks going off every time I'm within a few feet of the man I plan to spend the rest of my life with."

Jessie pressed the phone against her ear, certain she'd heard wrong. No fireworks with Mac? How was that possible? "Are you telling me there's no chemistry between you and Mac? None at all?"

"Well, there's some. I mean, I'm attracted to Mac. Who wouldn't be, but let's face it, if the 'can't keep my hands off you' chemistry was there, we would've already slept together."

"And here I was hoping that *if* you hadn't had sex yet it was because you love him and wanted to wait until after you're married."

Jenna chuckled. "Oh, Jessie, you really are a true romantic. I waited because Mac has women throwing themselves at him all the time. He would never have proposed if I'd already slept with him."

Jenna had always liked games.

"Wait a minute. You're telling me that you think the only reason Mac proposed is because you played hard to get?"

"Of course not. But a little mystery never hurts."

"But aren't either of you in love with each other?"

"Love rarely lasts, anyway. Look at the divorce statistics. Mac and I have something more solid—mutual respect and shared goals."

"If you really believed that, you wouldn't be with Dylan. And if you and Mac don't love each other, what's in it for either of you to marry?"

"Mac gets his dream girl, a babe with a brain who will work as hard as he does. And marriage to Mac will give me more of what I want and quicker. Being his wife as well as a partner in the firm will instantly enhance my status, which means access to the higher profile cases. He's a big shot in this town and I'll be right there in the spotlight with him."

"Then what on earth are you doing with a drummer who's always broke and the only spotlight he'll ever be in is the strobe light of some nightclub? Do you love *him?*"

Jenna laughed. "Get real. We have nothing going for us but chemistry and the last couple of days have convinced me that's definitely not enough. So meeting up with Dylan was actually a good thing."

"If you say so. At least that means you've gotten him out of your system for good. Give me your flight number and I'll pick you up tomorrow."

"I had to cancel it. I had a—"

"Jenna, I don't want to hear it. You need to come home."

"I know, and I will. Just as soon as the swelling goes down. I had an allergic reaction to some eye cream that I had to buy since I left town unexpectedly and didn't have any of my own stuff. My face is all swollen and I look seventy years old. I can't go out in public, let alone get on an airplane."

Jessie knew her image-conscious sister well enough to know that wasn't a battle worth fighting. "How long?"

"I'm not sure. Soon, I hope. Can you cover for me just a few more days? Please?"

Jessie knew it'd take more than a few days for her to wrap her mind around the fact that her sister went all starry-eyed over a vagabond drummer and had only a lukewarm reaction to Mac, the supposedly perfect man for her. "Jenna, you don't know what you're asking. We're all supposed to have dinner with Mom and Dad tonight. I'd never fool them. And you've said so yourself that Mac is extremely intelligent. He's bound to catch on."

"Damn. I hate it when you're right."

"Besides, I had a fight with Mac last night, so I'm obviously not good at being you."

"You and Mac had a fight? That's odd. It's pretty hard to ruffle his feathers. What was it about?"

"It's a long story, but he wanted to make sure I, I mean you, hadn't changed your mind about having kids. He was very adamant about not wanting a family. Do you know why?"

"No, but then it was never a big deal to me because I don't have a maternal bone in my body." Jenna paused. "I don't feel right about you telling Mac that you were pretending to be me yesterday. He's going to feel like he's been played for a fool and he won't be a happy camper."

Jessie shivered. Mac was obviously a proud man and she doubted he'd find anything about her charade amusing. However, she'd survived his irritation before and would find a way to placate his bruised ego. "I'm not looking forward to it, but it beats trying to keep up the deception."

"Will you at least not tell Mac where I've gone or why? He can be relentless and I just can't face all his questions right now."

"Jenna, this isn't right. You're not being fair to either man."

"I'm not sleeping with Dylan, if that's what you're thinking. He's leaving town tonight, and even if he wasn't, it wouldn't matter. Mac is the man I want to marry."

Jessie let out a sigh of relief over the discovery of one positive in the midst of so many negatives. "So, what are your plans?"

"I've checked into the spa and am going to see if they can come up with some treatment that will help the swelling go down quicker."

Jessie's brain and stomach protested against delaying the inevitable, but the bond they shared as twin sisters was simply too strong to ignore. "All right. But the longer you stay away, the more you risk losing everything, Jenna."

"I knew I could count on you, sis. You're the best. Bye."

Jessie hung up the phone and stared into space with one ridiculous thought going through her mind—Jenna and Mac didn't have the hots for one another.

Jessie should've been berating herself for agreeing to do her sister's dirty work and confessing to Mac about the deception, or worrying about how she'd handle his angry reaction to the news.

At the very least, she should feel guilty for the instant pleasure she had felt at the prospect of spending more time with Mac. Instead, all she could think about was Jenna's shocking admission over the lack of chemistry between her and Mac, the perfect man for her in every other way.

Jenna's confession blew a hole in Jessie's theory of why she reacted so strongly to Mac's presence. She had assumed that she had simply been responding to a pre-existing sexual tension between the engaged couple.

Now she didn't know what to think. Mac wasn't her type and was off-limits for too many reasons to count, yet the most innocent touch affected her more than another man's skilled seduction.

Why she reacted to Mac at all didn't matter, Jessie reminded herself. In six days he was marrying her sister. End of subject.

Mac rang Jenna's doorbell at ten o'clock Sunday morning, then knocked. He probably should've called first, but he didn't want to take the chance she'd refuse to talk to him. He had to assure himself that she was okay. The memory of her distraught, sad expression before she'd vaulted from his car had haunted him all night.

He also wanted to tie up some loose ends. He should never have allowed her to leave the car before he'd presented his "case" with the facts to back up his decision for not wanting children. But he hated talking about the past, opening old wounds that still felt raw.

The door opened. "Mac, I'm glad you're here. We need to talk."

A surge of relief hit Mac with such a force it left him stunned. He brushed aside the odd sensation and focused on her, instead. Makeup covered most of the shadows under her eyes, but not all. She obviously hadn't gotten much sleep, either, and it was his fault. Damn. He could be a jerk sometimes. "I know. I overreacted last night and I want to explain why."

"I need to tell you something, too, Mac. I—"

"No, let me go first. This is important." He guided her to a chair at the kitchen table then pulled another chair over to sit across from her. Her hands lay folded in her lap and he covered them with his own. "I never talk about this subject if I can help it, but on the drive home last night I realized that you'll be meeting my mother soon and she'll no doubt bring it up and you should be prepared."

"Mac, listen to me—"

"My younger brother died from a rare form of cancer when he was fourteen," he blurted out, intent on revealing the painful memory then quickly packing it away again in the far recesses of his mind.

Jenna's eyes widened and her hands unfolded to grip his. "I'm so sorry."

"Luke had stopped responding to accepted treatments so we were trying an experimental one, his last hope, and we knew he didn't have much time left. My mom was amazing through the whole thing. She always tried to make our lives seem as normal as possible, even during the worst times."

And his brother had been so brave, so strong as he lay in the hospital bed connected to a dozen tubes. Mac could almost smell the antiseptic, hear the pumps and machines working diligently to keep Luke alive.

"Mac, what happened?"

Mac shook off the vivid memory. "As if the poor kid didn't have enough to deal with, his appendix burst and what should've been a routine surgery ended up killing him. We lost what little time we might have had with him because his surgeon was using drugs."

"That's why you specialize in personal injury cases."

He nodded. "After Luke died, the insurance company took advantage of my mom's situation, knowing she was a grieving single parent and wouldn't have the energy to keep after them to do the right thing. God knows I wanted to help her then, but I couldn't. So, I help others now. Doctors, hospitals and insurance companies must be held accountable."

"And you're involved with C.D.R. because of your brother."

"Well, it's always good for public relations to back a worthwhile charity." He didn't want to mislead her into thinking he was some altruistic saint; he'd simply chosen one that helped other kids who suffered the way his brother had.

"But what does any of this have to do with you not wanting to have children of your own? You obviously have a good relationship with your mother and it sounds like she did a wonderful job parenting under very stressful circumstances."

He couldn't argue with that assumption, but watching his brother suffer had convinced him that he didn't want to take the chance of being a parent who lost a child. "My job is my life. It wouldn't be fair to the kid or me."

Jenna put her hands on his cheeks, her fingers cool to the touch. Clear, caring green eyes shimmered with unshed tears. "One man, no matter how amazing, can't right all the wrongs. You deserve to have a life, too."

Her unexpected compassion unnerved him. Why wasn't she agreeing with him like always about work being a priority? Why did he feel compelled to kiss the sad smile from her beautiful face?

Without a conscious thought, he leaned forward to do just that.

Suddenly, her hands slid from his face and pushed against his chest. "Wait, Mac, there's something I have to tell you."

The worry in her gaze and urgency in her voice stopped him cold, but like an overheated, misfiring engine, his body temperature continued to spike and his heartbeat grew erratic.

What the heck had just happened? He'd never gotten so worked up over a kiss from Jenna before, why so hot and bothered over an almost kiss now?

Something wasn't right about his fiancée, hadn't been right since yesterday morning, but what was he missing?

He leaned back in his chair and folded his arms across his chest as he studied her. Her long blond hair was uncharacteristically pulled back in a common ponytail, her makeup less dramatic than usual. And instead of tying the denim work shirt at the waist to tease him with a flash of her flat stomach, the shirttails hung loose over designer blue jeans.

Yesterday's inconsistencies suddenly made sense. "I'll be damned. You're not Jenna."

Chapter Four

The imposter held out her hand, signaling him to stop. "You're right. You were dealing with me, not Jenna, all day yesterday. I tried to tell you the minute you arrived, Mac, but you wouldn't listen."

Mac opened his mouth to protest, but what could he say? He'd been so hell-bent on telling her about his brother so he could get it over with and never have to mention the painful subject again, that he'd ignored her attempts to interrupt him.

Still, he resented being played for a fool; she wasn't completely off the hook. "I suppose you're going to tell me that it was all some twin thing, a test to see if the unsuspecting fiancé can tell you apart?"

"Don't be ridiculous."

"That's rich. What do you call what you pulled last night?"

Jessie reached for a small bottle of antacid on the table and popped two in her mouth. "Jenna is feeling stressed over the wedding, but it's nothing to worry about. She asked me to fill in for her final dress fitting, said she'd be back in town the next morning, so I didn't see any harm. But then you showed up at the bridal shop and things just snowballed from there."

"So why not tell me this before we left for the fundraiser? Unless making fools of people is something twins do for laughs."

She curled her hands into fists. "I hated pretending, but I'd promised Jenna. She was only supposed to be gone for the day and didn't want to make you worry."

"I hope you realize that I would've seen right through you if Jenna hadn't already been acting so strange."

"Of course. The Jenna we know would never be undecided on a wedding dress, let alone forget a meeting with a client."

The realization he'd been duped acted like a pinprick to his ego; doubt trickled in over Jenna's commitment to marrying him. "Maybe she's changed her mind and she can't face calling off the wedding at the last minute."

Jessie shook her head. "Jenna isn't afraid of anything, never has been. She just needs some time alone before the big day."

He stood and paced the concrete floor. Something wasn't right, but until he spoke with Jenna directly, he only had the reassurance of a biased third party. He preferred cold, hard facts. "Did Jenna say when she might return?"

"Not exactly, but it shouldn't be more than a few days."

"So what do we do about dinner tonight with your parents? Surely you're not going to try and fool them, too."

"Of course not. When I realized Jenna wasn't going to be back in time, I told her that I couldn't keep her absence a secret any longer."

"I guess I'll call your parents, then, and cancel for the both of us." Which meant he'd need to clear a night for dinner during the week, since he and his in-laws were more or less starngers, and being thrown together at the rehearsal Friday night could prove awkard. Providing there would still be a rehearsal dinner.

Jenna better have a good reason for playing havoc with his work schedule.

"If you do that, they might suspect something is wrong. They're so happy about the wedding and they're really looking forward to getting to know you better, since there wasn't any time to visit at the couples shower. They have this elaborate meal already in the works."

"What do you suggest?"

"The two of us can still go. I'll let them know that Jenna's come down with something, which isn't really a lie, and she insisted we go without her. We can meet there. Do you need directions to the house?"

The solution freed up his evenings for work, and he saw no reason to get off on the wrong foot with his future in-laws, but it didn't help solve the mystery behind his fiancée's absence.

He suspected Jessie knew more than she admitted. If he had the time, he might be able to earn her trust, get her to confide in him. "You live in west Plano, right?"

She nodded.

"Then my condo can't be that far from you. There's no point in us both driving," he said, confident he would have his "witness" confessing all she knew during the ride to her parents' home. "Write down your address for me and I'll pick you up at five."

Mac parked in front of Jessie's place, a small red-brick house with black shutters. The traditional one-story in the suburbs couldn't have been more different from Jenna's downtown loft apartment.

So what? He was stalling and knew it. A nagging sense of guilt left him hesitant to get out of the car, which irritated him even more.

Why should it matter that he had a hidden agenda for insisting they ride together to her parents' house? He had a right to know what was going on with Jenna. The drive would provide time alone to pump her sister for more information.

As for the voice in his head that continued to remind him of his overreaction to the almost-kiss that morning, well, he couldn't be held responsible since he'd thought Jessie was his fiancée at the time.

Except, deep down, he worried that a part of him had known the truth, or at least suspected, all along.

But the subterfuge had ended, and now he was simply taking his future sister-in-law to meet his future in-laws.

So get out of the car already.

He eased his frame out of the small vehicle and was immediately hit with a wave of late afternoon heat. His long-sleeve button-down shirt and dress slacks weren't as hot as a suit, but still plenty uncomfortable.

Thank God for air-conditioning.

He quickly made his way up the sidewalk. To the left of the front door was a large bay window, to the right a long front porch that no doubt benefited from the shade of a huge oak tree a few feet away.

The soothing sound of trickling water caught him off guard. He scanned the property until he located a fountain tucked between bushes.

Pastel-colored flowers in pots of varying colors and sizes dotted the porch floor and hung from baskets. A padded glider placed beneath ceiling fans beckoned him to take a seat, relax. He had no idea they even made gliders anymore.

She might as well have a huge sign flashing Welcome, although it would've been redundant.

The front door opened before he had a chance to knock.

"Hi, Mac. Come on in."

Jessie appeared much more relaxed now, no doubt because she was back to being herself and in more comfortable surroundings.

Damn, but she was beautiful.

A white sundress revealed tanned, toned arms and long legs. Toes painted the color of lilacs peeked out of flat sandals.

Once again he was struck by the dissimilarities between the identical twin sisters. Jenna, in the same outfit, would've looked entirely different because of the flashy jewelry she favored and the high heels she always wore. The only accessory Jessie sported, a pair of dainty diamond studs, made her ears appear incredibly sexy.

"Mac, I promise I'll only be a minute. Won't you come inside?"

What was wrong with him? He'd never given any woman's ears a second thought before, let alone found them sexy. And she was his future sister-in-law, for crying out loud. "Sure."

The whole twin thing was playing with his head, he reasoned. If he noticed or reacted to anything about Jessie, it was only because she looked so much like Jenna. He'd proposed to Jenna, the perfect woman for him.

He stepped into the foyer that opened out into a spacious room with big, comfortable-looking furniture. The scent of lilac filled the air, reminding him of his glimpse of her polished toes. She must enjoy the smell as well as the color, he guessed, then reprimanded himself for such fanciful thinking.

In search of a distraction, he studied the living room. Green plants with shiny leaves topped off bookcases that lined one wall. Knickknacks, more plants and books were interspersed with framed black-and-white photos on the various shelves.

His uneasiness grew at the thought that the inside of the house proved as inviting as the outside. Unlike his minimalist approach to decorating and Jenna's loft, which bore the stamp of a high-priced decorator, this wasn't just a house, it was a home.

"I need to put out some birdseed then I'll be set to go," Jessie said over her shoulder as she walked away.

He followed her down a short hallway and into the

kitchen. A stone wall boasted a fireplace, adding a rustic charm and coziness to the large, open room. The fading late afternoon sun trickled in through the French doors. "Birdseed?"

"I like to watch the birds while I have my coffee and read the paper in the morning. It's relaxing, not to mention at times downright entertaining."

She opened a cupboard, removed the lid of a big plastic tub and filled a large scoop with birdseed. "The birds are used to my feeding them in the afternoons when I get home from school, so I keep up the routine even when I'm not working."

He opened the sliding door for her, but remained in the air-conditioned kitchen as she stepped out onto a patio.

"Just leave the door open, Mac. I won't be long."

The sound of wind chimes tickled the air as she made the rounds to three birdfeeders hanging from a large tree, then fetched a watering can and added water to a birdbath.

He stood in the doorway, mesmerized by her graceful movements and the obvious delight she took from performing each simple task.

She met his gaze and smiled. "It's a shame it isn't closer to nightfall. The cardinals are my late diners and my favorite, although blue jays are a close second. Have you ever seen a baby blue jay?"

"Not that I recall." But then, he didn't spend much time gazing out windows. "The only birds I see are sparrows when I'm driving." Ugly, nasty birds.

"I get those, too, but you'd remember if you had ever seen a blue jay fledgling. They look bald because their feathers haven't popped out yet and it's so comical. Anyway, the parents fly with their baby—which is almost as big as an adult—into my backyard for dinner and the whole time the baby is squawking and flapping its wings until the parents feed him some of the birdseed."

Her smile grew wider as she shook her head and chuckled at the memory. "Sometimes, I get so caught up watching the birds that my coffee grows cold and the paper doesn't even get read."

He couldn't imagine wasting time in such a frivolous fashion, even on a weekend, but for some reason, coming from her, the notion tempted him more than he cared to admit.

No way. Not him. The mellow surroundings were just getting to him. After all, the inside of the house was just as serene and welcoming as the outside.

Damn, he was losing it, no doubt from all the extra hours he'd put in recently to clear his desk for the weeklong honeymoon. As much as he hated to admit it, the break from work might do him some good, but truth be told, he'd planned on taking at least *some* work along. He wouldn't be surprised if Jenna had the same idea.

Jessie returned, tucked the scoop away in the bucket and washed her hands. "See, it didn't take long at all."

Good. He had no interest in being relaxed or entertained by birds or their caretaker.

She picked up a large gift bag from the table along with her purse and led the way to the front door.

"I just brought a bottle of cognac for your parents. Is it someone's birthday?"

"No, nothing like that. This is a gift for our house-keeper's grandson. He's getting baptized today."

"That would be Martha, right? Jenna's mentioned her before, how she practically raised you." But he doubted Jenna kept up with the help's personal life.

Jessie nodded. "She was, is, wonderful. It's a shame you won't meet her today, but she'll be at the wedding, and at the house for all the other Sunday dinners."

Jessie must have gotten her nurturing tendencies from Martha, then, since Jenna claimed both parents were distracted, somewhat distant geniuses.

He glanced at his watch. "We'd better get going." He dreaded being late almost as much as he hated to be kept waiting by others.

"Do you go anywhere without it?" Jessie asked as she locked up the house and walked with him to his car.

"Without what?"

"Your watch."

"Why would I do that? I'm a lawyer. Everything is done by the clock."

She shrugged her slender shoulders. "I refuse to clock-watch when I'm away from the classroom. Otherwise, I can't really relax and enjoy the moment."

"Well, work is what I enjoy, and I'd never get anything accomplished if I lost track of the time," he replied, intent on directing the conversation away from him and onto his absent fiancée. "And Jenna is the same way, but I guess you know that. Would you say that you and Jenna are pretty close?"

"Closer than some, less than others. Do you ever drive with the top down?"

Mac did a double take. He preferred the open air, but Jenna hated it. "Sure. But it's still too hot." Not to mention the whipping wind would make conversation—the whole point of this drive—difficult.

Once they were both belted in, Jessie gave him directions to the general area of her parents' house. He headed for the tollway, the quickest route to the older neighborhoods of Dallas.

The scent of her perfume reminded him of the flowers on her porch, subtle yet sexy and very distracting. "So the fact that you two are so different doesn't get in the way of being close?" he asked, determined to remain focused. "You'd sense if Jenna were in some kind of trouble?"

Jessie fidgeted with her seat belt. "I talked with her and *know* she's okay. I don't need some kind of ESP to tell me that."

"Has she ever done anything like this before?"

"No, but she's never been engaged before, either. Let me put it to you this way—would you agree that in some ways Jenna thinks and acts more like a male? She's very direct, super competitive, logical."

"Yes. So?"

"Well, a guy will sometimes get a little crazy before the wedding when the reality of what a huge commitment marriage is hits him. He's about to promise to spend the rest of his life with one woman. One. But once he remembers all the reasons why she's perfect for him, how empty his life will be without that one woman, he knows he's ready for marriage." Jessie paused. "I wouldn't be surprised if that's what happened to Jenna."

"You seem to be making a lot of assumptions. You can't be sure."

"No, but she made a point of telling me that she *is* sure about marrying you. After a little downtime she'll come home and the wedding will go on as planned."

Jessie turned in her seat to face him. "Who's to say *you* won't be hit with a case of cold feet sometime before the wedding Saturday night?"

He shook his head. "I don't waste time second-guessing myself. Once a decision is made, I run with it."

Sunday afternoon traffic proved light on the tollway and soon they had crossed under LBJ Freeway. Jessie gave him more specific directions to her family home off Forest Lane.

Damn. He wasn't getting anywhere with Jessie. She was obviously very loyal to her sister, a trait he admired, but for selfish reasons in this case, also cursed.

"I don't know what Jenna has told you about our parents," Jessie said. "But there's nothing traditional about them. Our dad is a research scientist. He's extremely absentminded and logical about everything but the Dallas Cowboys. Growing up, it was the only thing he and his father had in common, so Dad is a little fanatic. Just agree with whatever he says about the team and you'll do fine."

Jessie paused for a breath. "Mom is the dean of economics at Southern Methodist University and more ambitious than many men. She'll try to draw me into an argument about my job, but just ignore her and let me handle it. Oh, and don't expect a home-cooked meal, just an excellent one. Neither of my parents cook, but Henri, he's our chef, comes to the house every Sunday morning and prepares dinner and enough meals to get them through the week."

"That explains Jenna's aversion to the kitchen, which probably means you're a gourmet chef."

Jessie's laughter filled the contained space of his sweet machine. "I do like to cook, but just your plain old meat and potatoes and pasta dishes."

"Is there *anything* you and Jenna have in common outside of looking alike?"

"We both play a mean game of tennis, but I usually let Jenna win because she's a terrible loser. Although I'll deny it if you tell her that."

"I doubt she'd believe you anyway." Jenna's confidence was one of the things he found most attractive about her.

Jessie chuckled. "You're probably right." She pointed to the house on the corner. "Just pull into the circular driveway."

Mac let out a whistle of appreciation for the two-story Mediterranean-style home. An alcove with a curved wrought-iron railing perched above double front doors. Massive trees shaded the driveway. "Now I know where Jenna got her taste in houses."

"Houses, cars, clothes," Jessie added. "There's nothing subtle about Jenna. That's probably one of the things that attracted you to her, right?"

"Right." At least that had been the case until he met Jessie, who had taught him subtlety could be unbelievably sexy.

But he wasn't worried. So what if he'd discovered he was attracted to more than one type of woman? Since he never intended to act on it, the matter proved irrelevant. Case closed.

Jessie hurried out of the small but powerful car, eager to put distance between herself and Mac. His third degree regarding Jenna's absence had put her on edge. Jessie would hate to face him in court.

Even worse, though, was how his sexy cologne affected her hormones. Her brain knew he was out of bounds, so why wouldn't her body cooperate?

She rang the doorbell. Within seconds, the door opened and Henri held out his arms for their traditional hug. His handlebar mustache tickled her cheek and triggered pleasant childhood memories.

"Ms. Jessie!" He held her at arm's length to look at her. "And how is my chef extraordinaire?"

She smiled. "I'm great, and you're much too kind." She motioned to Mac. "Henri, I'd like you to meet Jenna's fiancé, Mac McKenna."

The men shook hands. "Congratulations, Mr. McKenna, and welcome. But where is Ms. Jenna? I prepare this meal in her honor, all of her favorites."

Henri would probably detect a lie quicker than her parents, so Jessie again decided to stick as close to the truth as possible. "Jenna would be here if she could, Henri."

Jessie stepped inside the house with the men following close behind her. The unmistakable aroma of roasting lamb and fresh-baked bread left her mouth watering and her stomach growling. "I'll be sure and let Jenna know how wonderful everything was."

Jessie deposited her purse and gift bag on the marble-topped table in the center of the expansive foyer.

"And I'll fix a plate for you to take to her, yes?"

"That would be great. Mom and Dad in their usual corners?" she asked, even though she already knew the answer.

Henri nodded. "I will inform them that you are here."

She turned to Mac. "Don't take it personally that they didn't greet you themselves. They stay immersed in their work until forced to join the rest of the world."

"Trust me, I'm the last person who would be offended."

Of course. What had she been thinking? Still, a naive part of her had thought that meeting their future son-in-law would've offered enough incentive to make an exception. "That was how the Sunday family dinner tradition started," she offered as she led the way into the opulent formal dining room.

The exquisite cherry table and chairs shined from a recent polishing. She imagined that Mac shared her parents' and Jenna's preference for the calculated perfection only a high-priced decorator could provide. "Months would go by without all of us ever being in the same room together, so for the past ten years, at least once a week on Sundays we play catch-up."

Although Jessie was in favor of the tradition, it often felt like a substitute for the everyday closeness she knew other families experienced.

She loved her parents and accepted their limitations when it came to giving of themselves, but someday she would have an old-fashioned family who was involved in each other's lives, who had dinner together on a regular basis on a sturdy table in a cozy kitchen.

Her mother appeared, dressed in an elegant cream-colored pantsuit and wringing her hands. "Oh, Jessie, thank goodness you're here. Martha never showed up today of all days. And she knew we were having guests."

Jessie gave her mother the customary kiss on either cheek. "Martha asked for this weekend off a month ago, remember? She had family coming in for her grandson's baptism today."

"Well, she could've at least come by for a few hours. She knows that I don't know where anything is. Dinner will be late if—"

"I'll go give Henri a hand in a minute," Jessie assured, then motioned to Mac. "Mother, say hello to the guest of honor. I know you've been looking forward to seeing him again."

Mac offered his hand, which her mother shook then clasped with both of her hands for a few seconds. "Welcome, Mac, and please, forgive me. It's been a rather stressful morning, but I'm thrilled to have this chance to get better acquainted."

"The pleasure is mine, Mrs. Taggert. Jenna mentioned you and your husband are fond of cognac after dinner." He held out the bottle wrapped in a black silk bag.

Her mother smiled and suddenly looked years younger. "A man who pays attention. How delightful and rare. I dearly love the girls' father, but he's usually in another world." Her mother's smile faded. "It's so unfortunate that Jenna couldn't come tonight. You told me she's sick, but it's nothing serious. Are you sure?"

"Positive," Jessie assured. "She's just a little under the weather." Nursing her cold feet. Jessie had to swallow her resentment toward her sister for putting her in the position of telling half-truths to their parents and Mac, who would soon be part of their family.

"I'll call her later, then, just to see how she's doing."

"Okay, Mom, but don't worry if she doesn't answer. She told me she was going to turn the ringer off and sleep most of the day."

Her father then entered the room. Tall and thin, he wore his standard uniform—a wrinkled button-down shirt and khakis along with a befuddled expression on his narrow face. "What's all the commotion? I can't hear myself think."

When he spotted Jessie, his eyes lit up. "I'd already forgotten—it's Sunday!" He rushed toward her with arms wide and she stepped into his bear hug. "It's about time you came to see your old man, Jessie-girl."

"I missed you, too, Dad."

"Well, introduce me to your friend, here." He nodded at Mac. "It's good to see you're dating again."

"Uh, no, Dad, he isn't—"

"I'm Mac McKenna, Jenna's fiancé," Mac thankfully interrupted. "We only met briefly at the couples shower last month, sir."

The puzzled expression returned to her father's face as he shook the offered hand. "Of course. Sorry. Honest mistake. I mean, you're standing next to Jessie, not Jenna, so naturally... Where is Jenna?"

How could anyone, even a man as preoccupied as her father, think Mac was her type? "Fill Dad in, Mom. I'll go see if Henri needs any help."

"That would be wonderful." Her mother gave Jessie the cognac, then took her father by the arm, offered the other to Mac and led the way into the dining room. "I'll tell you what I know about Jenna, dear, while we take our seats. And Mac, it's Deborah and Lee. No sense in being formal with family."

Jessie hurried toward the safety of the kitchen where no one would confuse Mac for her date.

Several minutes later, Jessie had collected the serving pieces from the buffet table. She assisted Henri with transferring the food to the dining room table and then took her seat across from Mac.

The empty chair next to him might as well have been a flashing neon sign that spelled out the word "deceit." Jessie hated dodging the truth and hoped Jenna would soon come clean with Mac about where she'd gone and why.

Jessie's appetite waned, but she forced herself to take a few bites of the lamb and roasted red potatoes covered in rosemary and olive oil.

"So, Mac," her mother said. "Jenna tells me The French Room was booked for your rehearsal dinner so she went with her second choice, La Grande Maison. I hope you're not too disappointed."

He shook his head. "Jenna has impeccable taste. I've left all the details up to her."

"Very smart," Jessie's father piped in. "But let's talk

about something a man really cares about. How do you think the Cowboys will do this year?"

Mac shrugged. "I've never been a big fan of football, or 'America's Team.' I'm more of a hockey guy myself."

Not *too* smart, apparently, Jessie decided. She kicked Mac under the table, but he simply grinned. Meanwhile, the confused expression had returned to her father's face as he put down his fork and knife.

"Does Jenna know this?"

"Frankly, sir, the subject never came up. But she has been to a Stars game. Of course, she was a little more interested in seeing herself on the JumboTron and networking than watching hockey, although she didn't seem to mind the game itself."

"Well, the Stars better draft some youth and speed if they hope to win the Stanley Cup again," Jessie offered without thinking.

Mac's jaw dropped. He raised his eyebrows. "They won the cup with the old guys, didn't they?"

"Kids," Jessie's mother interrupted. "Enough sports talk, please. Now, the wedding is just six days away. We have lists to go over. Everything must be perfect for Jenna."

Her mother reached for Jessie's hand resting on the table. "I just wish my other daughter was settled. I worry so. You don't get out enough. Maybe if you were on staff at a university, you'd have a better chance at meeting someone."

Jessie always marveled at her mother's persistence. "Mom, I have no interest in dealing with adults who already have their minds made up about everything, and it hasn't been that long since I broke things off with Robert. When I'm ready, I promise I'll dive right back into the dating pool."

"Robert was too young for you, anyway," her father piped in. "But you're certainly old enough to know where you want to go with your career. Don't you want to at least advance? I thought you were going after a principal position."

Since age had been the main issue with Robert, she didn't bother to protest. He hadn't been looking for anything serious, and justly so, but she wanted more than fun times at this point in her life. "I'm looking into it, Dad, but it's just not the right time," Jessie replied, although she couldn't say why, especially when she knew that lately she'd been feeling more restless than usual.

Still, when the time had come to sign up for continuing education courses, she had opted for the usual, instead of the mid-management certification classes required to pursue the job of principal.

"The role of a principal is an important one, obviously," Mac said. "But I don't think you can overestimate the importance of good teachers for the younger kids." He calmly took a drink of wine as if he'd made some throwaway comment on the weather.

Did Mac have a short memory or was he merely insane? Didn't he care at all about making a good impression with his future in-laws? She kicked him again, but his attention remained on her mother.

Her mother pressed her lips together, her father glared. The last time Jessie had witnessed such disapproval from her parents was when she'd announced her career choice.

"Without the best teachers when they're young," Mac added, "those kids might never even graduate from high school, let alone make it to college."

He turned to Jessie and smiled but she refused to let him see how his rushing to her defense had touched her. Nothing good could come of him realizing that she was beginning to see him more like a sexy, self-possessed champion of the underdog instead of a bossy workaholic.

She'd already weakened this morning when he'd confessed the tragic reason behind why he had made his work his life, and now he'd butted in and defended her choice of a career to her parents.

How could Jenna *not* be attracted to, let alone be in love with, such a man? Maybe in time she'd grow to love him. Jessie hoped so.

Meanwhile, she needed to clarify a point to her future brother-in-law. "Mac, thanks for the kind words, but this is an ancient debate. Mother knows that it's my decision, my life."

She stood. "I'll get the coffee and dessert."

"I'll help," Mac offered.

"No, you're the guest," she insisted, but he was already out of his chair and heading her way. Did the man ever take no for an answer?

Once behind the kitchen door she busied herself arranging the silver coffeepot and delicate porcelain cups on the serving tray. She made a mental note to remember to take the plate of food Henri had fixed for Jenna before he'd made a quiet exit from their home, as was the custom.

Jenna. Her sister should've been at the dinner, was probably the only person who stood a chance of keeping Mac in line. "Do you think it's a good idea to pick a fight with my parents, your future in-laws?" she whispered.

"All I did was answer honestly."

She shook her head and handed him the silverware. The man had guts, she begrudgingly admitted. She preferred to avoid confrontation whenever possible, but he seemed to relish it, which was probably what made him such a successful lawyer.

"So, just how young was this Robert guy?"

She did a double take at the change of topics. "What does that have to do with anything?"

"Hey, I'm just making small talk, trying to get to know my soon-to-be sister-in-law better. But if it's too painful to talk about—"

"Robert was like that country song, old enough to know better, but too young to care. It was fun, it's over and we're still friends. Nothing painful about it whatsoever. Next subject."

"Are you *really* a hockey fan?" Mac asked.

"Well, yeah. One game was all it took."

He grinned and she warmed to the genuine pleasure reflected in his gaze, then immediately felt guilty. He was just being a guy; it was nothing personal.

Except that he wasn't just any guy, but her future brother-in-law and way, way off-limits. "I'm not suggesting you lie to my parents, but couldn't you have been a little less blunt?"

He shrugged. "I've never been into playing games. If Jenna accepts me as I am, why shouldn't your parents?"

With a sigh, Jessie handed him a tray of crepes with hot cherries jubilee and real whipped cream. He might be the best at closing arguments in the courtroom, but she doubted he had ever encountered anyone like her parents before. "You can't say I didn't warn you."

Chapter Five

"Are you sure you don't mind having the top down?" Mac asked as he drove through one of Dallas's older neighborhoods. Huge oak trees formed a canopy, something the younger city of Plano wouldn't possess for many years.

He had decided to take side roads home, not only for the scenery, but because he hoped the slower speeds would lull Jessie into a more confessional mood.

"Positive," Jessie replied. "But I thought you said it was too hot."

He shivered. "I'm a little chilled after the cold shoulder I got from your parents during dessert." Jessie had tried her best to fill the stony silences, but the word *awkward* failed to describe the past thirty minutes.

Jessie's laughter mingled with the warm night air. "I did warn you about their hot buttons."

"Yes, you did. But there's no point in pretending to be someone I'm not. In time, they'll accept me the way I am."

"I doubt it'll happen before the wedding, though. But there will be plenty of time once you're married." Jessie tilted her head back; the breeze lifted her hair from her shoulders.

"I've always enjoyed a challenge," he replied, then realized the statement was only partially true because even as he spoke, he resented how he had to fight the impulse to reach out and touch the blond strands that looked like silk. He should've said that he only liked some challenges, not the ones that sucker punched his willpower.

Damn. This was all Jenna's fault. Their wedding was in six days and he still had no idea where his fiancée was hiding out or even why she had left in the first place.

He wanted and deserved answers.

The drive to dinner had been a bust, but now he had one more chance to pump Jessie for information about her sister. But first, he needed to gain Jessie's trust. "So, what made you decide to become a teacher?"

"My fifth-grade teacher. She was challenging, inspiring. She made a huge impact on me and I like to think I might do the same for some other child."

"But, third grade? Aren't you still holding their hands, so to speak?"

Jessie turned her body toward him. He stole a glance and caught the sparkle of passion in her eyes. "It's a trade-off I'm more than willing to make. These kids are so open and energetic, so creative and curious. Of course, occasionally, you have a kid who's more challenging than others, but hey, if it were easy, they wouldn't pay me the big bucks!"

He laughed with her, impressed by her passion and sense of humor. After meeting the Taggerts, it was clear to him that Jenna had molded herself after her parents, while Jessie, with her warm, generous nature, held claim to the title of "black sheep." Sweet, yes, but not a pushover. She'd made it clear she hadn't needed his help defending her career choice to her parents.

"Believe it or not," she continued, now somber, "I'd rather deal with a difficult child in the classroom than put up with some of the illogical, constrictive policies that the administration comes up with."

He asked her for an example and she offered several. "Those sound like reasonable complaints," he said. "Why doesn't someone do something about it?"

"It's complicated."

"If it's important, it can be figured out. Is that why you want to become a principal, so you can get into a position where you can affect change?"

"That's certainly part of it."

"So what's the holdup?"

"Why do you care? And besides, didn't I just hear you defend my choice of teaching?"

"Sure, and I meant every word. But if you're serious about being a principal, you shouldn't let anything hold you back. If no one is willing to bite the bullet and fight for change, it'll never happen."

"I'll do it when the time is right. I still enjoy the special bond I form with my students in the classroom and don't want to give that up. As a principal, I'd be helping the kids, sure, but from a distance."

"Well, change usually doesn't come without a price. If you feel strongly about it, you should take action instead of waiting for someone else to do it."

She turned away from him and folded her arms over her chest. "And sacrifice a personal life, like you've done, on the chance I *might* be able to improve school policies?"

Mac wondered what had happened to sweet and funny. Well, she could criticize his choices all she wanted. *Someone* had to fight to make the medical and insurance companies accountable. He was damn good at his job and proud of it. "I admit change usually comes at a price, but I don't have any regrets."

"Good for you. But I'm going to have to give a career change a lot more thought. Right now, I'm not willing to give up something I love to fight what might be a losing battle."

Why did she assume she'd fail if she tried? He barely knew her and could tell she was a natural leader.

"Can you step on it?" she asked, her voice laced with irritation. "It's been a long day and I'm tired."

Damn. He'd gotten so caught up in the effort to help solve her career dilemma that his unwanted advice had ruined his chance to get on her good side and gain her trust. "No problem."

He cut over to the tollway and joined the other speeding motorists, annoyed with himself for losing focus, something that was happening much too often lately.

The entire purpose of playing taxi for Jessie had been

to pump her for details about her sister—his fiancée—
and he hadn't learned squat.

He'd failed to reach Jenna all weekend and suspected
she was purposely avoiding him, and today had proven
he couldn't count on her sister for any help.

Tonight, he'd keep calling Jenna until she picked up
the stupid phone and answered his questions herself.

Mac rubbed his eyes, dry from too little sleep after
countless failed attempts to speak directly with Jenna.
At dawn, he'd given up and gone into the office, only
to discover she'd left a message there, saying that of
course the wedding was still on and she'd be back in
town sometime before Friday.

He suspected Jenna was purposely playing phone
tag with him, since caller ID would've told her that he'd
phoned from the house last night, yet when she retuned
his call minutes later, she'd phoned the office instead of
the house. But why play games?

Unfortunately, the reason why he kept losing his focus
and had yet to get a jump on the usual Monday-morning
chaos had nothing to do with his absent fiancée.

By nine o'clock, he'd only managed to shuffle the
same piles on his desk he'd been moving around since
he'd met Jessie. His mind continually drifted back to his
last conversation with her.

It frustrated him that she lacked faith in herself. She
was obviously intelligent, passionate about her work
and sensitive—she appeared to be the only member of
her family who saw the hired help as people, too.

And something told him that she'd signed all the

Taggert names to the card for the baptismal gift for the maid's grandson, so he might as well add generous to the list.

Why did a woman more than capable of leading a cause hang back?

Even more disturbing, though, was the fact that after she'd made it clear she hadn't appreciated his unsolicited advice, he was thinking about her instead of his own work.

His office door opened and Taryn poked her head in. "Hey, Mr. Mac, I made some fresh coffee, since you drank a pot before any of us got here. Do you want some?"

The recent high-school graduate had offered to fill in as secretary for her mother who was recuperating from a badly sprained ankle. Since she'd been coming to the office after school the past ten years, she knew the routine pretty well.

"I think I'll pass, but thanks."

"Oh, yeah, line one is for you. Are you taking calls now?"

"Who is it?"

"She wouldn't say, but she insisted it was an emergency and that you'd want to talk to her."

No hope the caller was Jenna, then. "Thanks. I'll take care of it."

Taryn disappeared and he picked up the phone. "Hello."

"Oh, thank God you took my call."

He easily recognized Jessie's voice, found himself straining to hear every word and inflection. "What's wrong, Jessie?"

"I think we've got a problem, unless you know something I don't and Jenna is on her way home right now."

"She left a message here at the office and said she'll be back sometime before Friday."

"Then you've got a big problem."

He gripped the receiver. "What do you mean?"

"I happened to check Jenna's phone messages and there's one from someone who sounded very young named Taryn. She asked Jenna to stop by around noon, that something had come up at the office. But Jenna had already arranged to take the week off. What could be so urgent?"

He groaned. "I smell a rat. I've been told to keep *my* lunch hour clear, that it was the only time a new client could come in."

"Is that unusual?"

"Only when combined with what you've just told me. I'm guessing that, against my wishes, they're throwing some sort of surprise couples shower."

"Just work in the conversation sometime this morning that Jenna's out of town."

"Jenna told me and everyone here that she needed the week off to work on the wedding. If I say she's out of town, they'll suspect something is up. I need everyone here at the office focused if I'm going to be able to leave Saturday for a weeklong honeymoon. I won't have that distraction."

"It looks like you're going to have a disruption whether you want one or not."

"Yes, but I guess the shower is a necessary interruption. And a party on company time will be short and sweet. If Jenna is a no-show, the staff will be bugging me with questions the entire day."

"Then tell them she's sick. It worked with my parents."

"Then at least one of them would be at her apartment with a care package only to find no one home. The rumors would start and I won't have—"

"I know, I know. No distractions. But even if you could contact Jenna now, she probably couldn't make it back in time."

"No, but *you* could."

"Me? Oh, no. Once was more than enough. My stomach is still in knots from the last time."

"I don't like this any more than you, but Jenna is more than my fiancée, she's a partner in the firm. My staff cares about her and looks up to her. You don't want their opinion of her to change, do you?"

"Boy, you go right for the jugular, don't you?"

"I don't have time to play nice. One hour. That's all I'm asking. For Jenna's sake."

"All right, all right. I'll do it. Against my better judgment."

"You won't be sorry," he promised, then gave her a rundown on his staff, what they looked like, a job description and personal information that might come in handy.

"Thanks again, Jessie," he said, and hung up the phone, grateful and relieved. At least this time he would be in on the twin switch. He hadn't known what to think on Saturday when he'd walked in on her at the bridal shop and felt a sudden, surprising chemistry.

All Jessie needed to do was make an appearance at the office. He'd play the part of the eager fiancé and remain at her side, close but no touching since the woman did crazy things to his hormones.

He needed that problem like he needed one more thing to go wrong before the wedding.

Jessie paused at the front door to Mac's office a few minutes before noon and popped more antacids. As stressful as her life had been lately, she should buy stock in the company that manufactured the fruit-flavored chalky tablets.

She fussed with the collar of the white linen jacket and hoped the pantsuit, an outfit she considered super-dressy, was close enough to something her sister would wear to the office on her day off.

At least she knew the hair and makeup would pass inspection, since she'd been able to reach Dana and Carla in time to enlist their help once again.

The high heels hurt her feet and Jessie had no idea how her sister wore them so often. But the shoes proved a minor irritation compared to facing her sister's co-workers. Could she even pull it off? And why should she even try? She was still annoyed with how Mac had challenged her career choices, the way he'd made it sound as if she had taken the easy way out instead of following her passion.

He was wrong and besides, it was none of his business. Except that a tiny voice inside insisted that her reaction had proven too strong for there not to have been any truth to his opinion.

To keep from turning around and going back home, she had to remind herself once again that she wasn't doing this favor for him but for Jenna, who had better return soon.

Jessie took a deep breath and pasted on a smile before she opened the door and stepped inside. Wow. Too bad Mac had skipped over the part about the plush decor when he'd provided the layout of the office during their phone conversation.

The office looked like something that should be featured in a magazine spread on how to impress. But she was supposed to be Jenna, who had seen it a million times, so Jessie quickly hid her surprise.

A young woman with curly red hair stood up behind the front desk and smiled. "Hi, Ms. Jenna. Sorry you had to come in on your day off."

"You said it was important, Taryn. Any idea what it's about?" The words felt cold and awkward, but if Jessie hoped to pull off the ruse, she needed to heed Mac's advice.

He'd explained that while Jenna was on good terms with everyone, she wasn't the buddy-buddy type. Jessie needed to act a little aloof.

Taryn shuffled some papers on her desk and chewed on her bottom lip. "You'll have to ask Adam. He's waiting for you and Mr. Mac in the conference room. I hope he doesn't get stuck on the phone with that windbag, Mrs. Petersen."

Mac suddenly appeared, impeccably dressed in a charcoal-gray suit; his strong masculine presence complemented the dark, rich colors of the Harvey paintings that graced the walls.

"Taryn, what's the rule around here concerning our clients?" he asked, his voice firm, but his expression patient.

Taryn rolled her eyes. "I know not to say anything mean if there's a client around. Ms. Jenna knows what a pain Mrs. Petersen can be, right?"

"Well, yes, but—" Jessie turned to Mac.

"Discussing clients in a negative way is a bad habit, Taryn," Mac offered. "You might slip when you don't mean to, so just watch it, okay?"

"I'll try." She cocked her head to the right. "You guys had better get to the conference room. Adam's waiting for you there."

Mac nodded, placed his hand on the small of Jessie's back, then quickly pulled it away as if burned. She felt a warm, tingling sensation where his fingers had fleetingly touched her, and she breathed a sigh of relief when his hand fell to his side as they walked down the hall.

Why did *this* man have to have the power to assault her senses whenever he was near? He was wrong for her in too many ways to count, the foremost being he was her future brother-in-law. Would she spend the next fifty years hiding her reaction to Jenna's husband?

Last night, after he had dropped her off, she had taken comfort in the fact that at least the stress of the masquerade was over and she could keep her distance from Mac.

Some distance. He was close enough for her to smell his sexy aftershave, feel the energy radiating from his body.

"You're doing great," he whispered, his breath on her ear causing her to shiver. "I owe you one."

"I'm doing this for Jenna."

"Whatever your reason, I'm grateful. I don't want my

staff worrying about the status of the wedding." He paused at the conference-room door. "They've gone to a lot of trouble, so remember to act surprised," he reminded, then turned the knob.

Jessie held her breath.

"Congratulations!"

"Surprise!"

A chorus of good wishes assaulted Jessie and Mac as they stepped inside.

Jessie didn't have to feign shock, but her astonishment had nothing to do with the surprise shower. No, what left her reeling was the discovery of Mac's protectiveness of his staff. His earlier grumbling had led her to believe his concerns involved eliminating distractions and rumors.

Taryn rushed in, apologizing for missing their entrance, but she had to stay behind to ensure they got to the room. She then proceeded to ask Jessie a million questions about the wedding dress, which, because she'd been at the final fitting, proved easy to answer.

How had one small favor created such a mess?

Mac remained by her side, but kept his hands stuffed in his pants pockets, for which she was grateful. She needed a clear head.

Champagne was poured and handed out. Jessie's protesting stomach prevented her from taking more than a polite sip and she prayed no one could sense her severe case of nervousness.

A short woman with curly red hair, no doubt Taryn's mother, hobbled over on crutches, exclaiming she wouldn't have missed the party for the world. She asked for details about the honeymoon with a twinkle in her blue eyes, the same shade as Taryn's.

Taryn hovered over her mother, insisting she sit down and follow doctor's orders. Mother and daughter shared many physical traits, but the obvious closeness between them made Jessie's throat tighten from an ache to someday experience that same bond with her own children.

Adam teased good-naturedly about whether Mac or Jenna would pull out their laptop first and how soon this would occur after the ceremony.

Regret washed over Jessie at the realization Mac and his staff were more like family than boss and employees; it made deceiving them that much more difficult.

"Hey, Mac," Adam called out. "Can I talk to you a second?"

"Sure."

Jessie thought Adam looked concerned, but couldn't imagine why. Mac shook his head at whatever question Adam had asked and relief swept over the young man's face as he punched Mac on the arm.

The men walked to the front of the room and stood behind a table laden with a cake and an elegant white gift bag stuffed with textured gold tissue paper.

Adam motioned for Jessie to join them. "Now it's time for the future bride and groom to practice feeding each other cake."

"Do what?" Mac asked.

"Mac, you have lots of great qualities, but finesse isn't one of them, right, Jenna?" Adam quipped, grinning.

"Good idea, Adam," Taryn chimed in. "You wouldn't want to risk ruining your wedding dress, Jenna."

Jessie glanced at Mac, assuming he would immediately squelch the idea.

Instead, he handed her the knife. "That sounds like a challenge to me." He met her gaze. "Shall we show them how it's done?"

He placed his hand over her trembling one, then cut two small pieces of the cake covered with cream-colored frosting and decorated with doves. Mac's and Jenna's names had been written in dark blue icing in honor of their wedding colors, antique white and navy. Different from the popular black-and-white theme, yet dramatic, which suited Jenna.

Mac picked up one piece and Jessie willed her hand to still as she followed his lead. What choice did either of them have?

"Ladies first," he said, his voice deep and husky.

Her stomach did flip-flops as she fed him the cake, then instinctively reached out to wipe frosting from the corner of his sensual mouth.

His gaze never leaving hers, he followed suit, then kissed her lightly on the lips. He tasted of sugar and champagne and she almost cried out at the unexpected tenderness of the much too brief kiss.

With her heart pounding in her ears, she barely heard the whistles and cheering. Lord, what was she doing? This was all pretend. He was her sister's fiancé. Guilt warred with the desire to know how it would feel if he *really* kissed her.

"Now open the present!"

Jessie blinked, grateful to have been pulled away from such dangerous thoughts. She stared at the gift bag, relieved she didn't have to deal with unwrapping a box since her hands refused to quit shaking.

"It's heavy," Taryn said. "So be careful."

Jessie tugged at the tissue paper then pulled out a crystal candy dish. "It's beautiful. Thank you."

"That's not all," Taryn insisted, her voice excited. "Check inside."

"You guys really do have everything," Adam chimed in. "So we went for clever and useful."

Mac raised the lid and removed gift certificates for several restaurants that boasted a delivery service. He unfolded the attached note and read aloud. "'For those many late nights at the office.'" He grinned. "Very practical. I like it."

Jessie felt all eyes on her, and although she didn't buy into the workaholic lifestyle, her sister obviously did. "This won't just come in handy at the office, folks. In case you didn't already know it, I don't cook," she quipped in an attempt to keep the mood light.

Mac chuckled and nudged her. "Your turn to pick one."

Jessie chose one of two small acrylic frames. The one she picked contained a photo of Mac, obviously cut out from a newspaper. "'So you'll remember what the other one looks like!'" she read from the tag.

Laughter filled the room and Jessie joined in, but her thoughts drifted to how much she'd underestimated the role work would play in her sister's married life. The sad truth was crystal clear now.

She ignored her heavy heart and forced a wry grin. "I just hope my picture is better than this one, or I could be in trouble, people. He'll never come home."

Mac's chuckle joined the resulting laughter as his arm slid around her shoulders and pulled her close. She assumed the embrace was part of the act, but didn't care because she needed his strength in order to continue the charade.

"This has been great, guys, but it's time to get back to work."

Good-natured groans filled the room.

"You really pulled one over on us," Jessie added. "Taryn, I'm not mad at you anymore for making me come in on my day off."

Taryn started another round of hugs and best wishes from the staff.

Finally, Mac steered Jessie out of the conference room and into his office. He shut the door.

"That was the longest thirty minutes of my life." She sank into the closest chair and dug in her purse for a roll of antacid.

"Got any extra?" Mac looked as miserable as she felt. She handed him two tablets.

"Thanks." He chewed and made a face. "Orange chalk. Interesting taste."

"Hey, it calms my stomach. That's all I care about. So, do you think they suspected anything?"

He leaned against the edge of his desk. "No, but we had a close call. Adam thought we'd been fighting."

"Why?"

"Taryn mentioned how I pulled my hand away from you in the hallway, and in the conference room I kept my hands in my pockets."

Mac abruptly stood and walked over to the window,

his back to her. "Anyway, that's why I went along with the whole cake-cutting thing. And the kiss."

Her fingers flew to her lips. She could still taste him, feel the hum of desire flowing through her body.

"It's sort of ironic, isn't it?" he asked. "We were so focused on you playing your role, which you did perfectly, and I'm the one who messed up." He turned around and stared at his hands. "Do they watch my every move?"

"I'm sure they don't, but even I noticed how you always had your hand on Jenna's shoulder or waist at the couples shower I gave."

He raised his eyebrows. "You did?"

She nodded.

"Is that a bad thing?"

"No, of course not. It's just a little surprising. Not that many guys are so attentive."

He shrugged. "I guess I get it honest enough. My mother is the touchy-feely type, and considering my brother's situation, no one was stingy with hugs."

Lost in memory, Mac looked as if *he* could use a hug, but it couldn't come from her, even though her heart ached for the teenage boy who must have resented being helpless to protect his family. He was too vulnerable at the moment and she didn't trust herself.

At least now she understood why he wanted to marry a woman he respected and cared for but didn't love, why he never wanted to have children.

Mac had experienced real love and real loss, and had decided to live without intimacy because he couldn't bear losing someone else he loved.

But darn it, she didn't want reasons to soften toward him, couldn't risk letting down her guard. She wanted the brusque workaholic back, not this more relaxed person who treated his staff like family, another shocker.

Today had clarified more than one thing to Jessie—now that she knew how much her sister had to lose, she had no regrets over standing in for her during the surprise shower.

But after today, the pretending stopped.

Chapter Six

"Thanks for coming to my rescue, again, Jessie," Mac said as the hostess seated them in a corner table at a popular Tex-Mex restaurant. "If I don't show up with my fiancée at Reverend Miller's office in an hour, there won't be a wedding on Saturday. I wouldn't have bothered you if there had been any other way. I know you hate all this pretending."

What an understatement and what a mess, Jessie thought as she tugged at the linen napkin in her lap. She had barely recovered from the draining effects of yesterday's masquerade, and was already breaking the promise she'd made to herself about no more deception.

She felt as if she were being pulled even deeper into the web of deceit and worried she'd get tangled up in all the lies, trip over the half-truths.

Yet, she couldn't refuse Mac's plea for help now

that she cared about his happiness as well as her sister's. So, when he had insisted lunch was the least he could provide in return for her favor, she had agreed. They would need the extra time anyway to go over the anticipated questions the minister might ask, along with their answers.

And while she cursed her sister for putting her in a position where she now had to be less than truthful with a *minister,* and thought Jenna was being extremely selfish at the moment, even so, she didn't deserve to have her wedding canceled. "This isn't your fault, Mac," Jessie assured. "And since Jenna is conveniently not answering her phone, we're stuck."

The waiter arrived, took their orders, then disappeared.

"So, what's the plan?" she asked, grateful they had a somewhat secluded table.

"He might ask how we met, which you already know. Money might come up. Of course there's a prenup, stating in case of divorce we take only what we brought into the marriage. And it makes sense to keep our money separate."

Jessie frowned. The whole arrangement seemed so cold.

"What's wrong?"

She shrugged. "Nothing. A prenuptial agreement is pretty standard these days, I guess."

"It definitely is."

"And it makes sense to keep your money separate in case, well, if things don't work out."

"You're wrong if you think we're going into this thinking the marriage will fail. Keeping the money separate is just simpler, and what Jenna and I have agreed on. That's all that matters."

"You're right. It's none of my business, anyway."

He nodded and took a drink of his sweetened tea. "The only other thing I can think of that he might mention is the issue of children, and that's something else Jenna and I agree on."

At least now Jessie had a better understanding of why he didn't want to be a dad, and Jenna was too driven and high-maintenance to consider motherhood. "I promise to keep my opinions to myself."

He leaned back in his chair. "I hear the disapproval in your voice. Plenty of people marry who don't want children. Why is having kids so important to you?"

"I don't disapprove, I just can't relate. I've always had this dream of a big, close family. Growing up, I had friends who had all sorts of traditions that brought everyone close together all year long. My family has one tradition, the Sunday family dinner, and it's based on guilt."

Jessie also wanted a family who loved unconditionally, who respected your choices and dreams even if they couldn't understand them.

"Some families don't even have that."

"I know. I love my family and accept them as they are, but they'll never be able to give me what I want the most. And I'm fortunate that the staff at my school is like family. We celebrate weddings, births and birthdays, cry together over a loss. I hope to create that with a family of my own someday."

The waiter brought their food. The grilled onion,

pepper and chicken fajitas smelled heavenly, but the thought of what lay ahead nipped at her appetite.

She was also bothered by the fact that not once had the word love been mentioned, either by Mac today, or by Jenna during previous conversations.

Jessie still couldn't reconcile marrying for any reason other than love, but if that was the kind of marriage that would make her sister happy, Jessie intended to support it, even if it meant playing keep-away with the truth from a man of the cloth.

No harm could come of the deception; she had nothing to gain from it and was trying to ensure her sister's happiness. So, she really had no reason to feel guilty. Yeah, right.

A large group of young kids dressed in soccer uniforms swarmed the restaurant. Fortunately, they were seated on the other side of the room, or conversation would've been impossible.

Mac leaned forward. "I just had an idea."

"About what?"

"You know how you said that one of the things that keeps you from pursuing the job of principal is that you'd miss the regular interaction with the students?"

She blinked, thrown by the unexpected change in the direction of their conversation. "Well, yes, but—"

"You're a born leader, Jessie. Look at how you took charge at the fund-raiser the other night. Because of how you roped those kids in, we raised more money than ever before."

"I had no idea. That's great, but—"

"You could be a principal and coach a team or teach a class outside of the school. It's the perfect solution."

He didn't have a clue about the impact of daily interaction with the same kids, and his smug smile irritated Jessie to no end. "Coaching or teaching an occasional class wouldn't be the same."

She was good in the classroom. Comfortable. The children were open, accepting. A principal was more of a "teacher of teachers." What if she didn't enjoy that role as much?

"Besides, we're not here to discuss my career options," she reminded, intent on changing the subject. "What else do you think the minister might bring up? I don't want to be caught off guard."

An odd sense of déjà vu fell over Mac as he stepped inside the minister's paneled office, then he realized why. For some reason, he equated the interview with being sent to the principal's office when he was a teenager. Not a common occurrence, but often enough to know you were rarely summoned for a reward.

Of course, back then, he had usually been guilty of some misdeed, just like now. Coincidence? Not likely.

"I'm glad to finally meet you, Mac and Jenna." Reverend Miller shook hands all around. "I have to admit, even after you messengered your marriage license to my office after the second cancellation, I thought you two might be having doubts about getting married."

"Nothing like that, Reverend," Mac assured. "Just busy schedules."

"Good. Because I'm human enough to admit that

I'm looking forward to officiating in such a unique setting. How on earth did you come up with the idea of getting married at the Dallas Museum of Art?"

"It was the wedding planner's idea, right, Jenn?"

Jessie nodded. "Right. She suggested the DMA when I said I was looking for someplace exciting and different."

Reverend Miller pointed at the love seat against one wall. On either side, like sentinels, stood sad-looking, cheap ficus trees in wicker baskets. "You're going to be here awhile, since we're combining several sessions into one, so you might as well get comfortable."

Mac swallowed hard at the sight of the small couch. Jessie took a seat and he had no choice but to follow suit. Just as he suspected, though, their shoulders and knees touched.

No wonder it was called a love seat, he thought irritably. The last thing he needed was to be squished for any length of time against a woman who left him more frustrated than an indecisive jury.

Even more confusing was why that same woman packed such a wallop in a whisper of a kiss, why her slightest touch left him more fired up than a teenage boy in heat.

An elbow nudged his side. "Mac, the reverend thinks you're nervous, but you're not, right?"

"No. Of course not." Because at that moment, he decided to eliminate his source of worry. Jessie was not going to have an effect on him anymore. Through sheer will, he'd remain distant, remote, as if he'd erected an invisible shield between them.

"Believe me, this makes most couples nervous, although I'm not really sure why." The trim man with white hair and dressed in jeans and collared shirt pulled a chair over and sat in front of them. "But this won't hurt, I promise."

Mac hid his surprise at the informal tone of the meeting. He'd expected a cut-to-the-chase interview. He didn't want to be the reverend's buddy.

"So, have you decided whether or not you want to write your own vows?"

"No," Mac said. "Just do the usual."

"Okay. I got the fax with the details for the rehearsal and the wedding. Jenna, it looks like you've got everything covered. So, let's talk about the two of you as a couple. How did you meet, how long have you known each other, and what made you decide to marry?"

Mac felt Jessie tense next to him. Out of the corner of his eye he observed her clasp and unclasp her hands in her lap.

He hated seeing her so nervous; he reached for her closest hand in an attempt to reassure her as he explained how Jenna had been hired on as an intern four years ago and had proven herself worthy of being made a partner; how they had discovered that they were just as compatible outside the office, so he'd proposed. Since neither of them had seen a need for a long engagement, a July wedding seemed the perfect choice.

A slight squeeze of his hand let him know she appreciated the gesture. Thank God she had no way of knowing that between almost sitting on top of one another and now holding hands, his hormones had kicked into overdrive.

The minister nodded. "It's great you have your work in common, but you'll need couple time, too, where you leave the job behind and simply focus on each other. Do you share any hobbies, maybe sports, or do you like to travel?"

Mac's mind froze. Work was his hobby, his life.

"We'll probably take some weekend trips nearby," Jessie offered. "I've heard that Arkansas in the fall is pretty with the leaves changing, something we don't get much of in Texas."

This time he squeezed her hand in gratitude for saving him when his brain had locked.

"Hot Springs is supposed to be charming and full of history," she added. "The water from the springs supposedly has healing powers, but even if that's just a myth, it would still be fun to hike or shop then get pampered at one of the spas."

"Are you on board with that, Mac?"

"Sure. Why not?" he replied, then worried that lightning would strike him for lying to a minister.

Then again, if *Jessie* were his fiancée and she'd suggested the trip, he really would be all over the idea because of the way her eyes had lit up just talking about it.

Which probably meant he should be hit with something more lethal than lightning.

"Good. I assume you've discussed the subject of children?"

Mac tensed. "We're committed to our careers. It wouldn't be fair to have a child under those circumstances."

Reverend Miller glanced at Jessie, who remained silent.

"You're awfully quiet, Jenna. Is that how you feel, also? No biological clock ticking? No pressure from your parents for grandkids? Not that you should base your decision on that, but these are all facts to be considered."

Mac held his breath and prayed Jessie would keep her promise to only voice her sister's views.

"Because of the work we do, bad doctors are weeded out and hospitals and insurance companies are held accountable. I can't imagine a more rewarding and fulfilling job."

"But what if it seems less so down the road? Will that cause a problem?"

"Not at all. My sister intends to have lots of children, so I'll have the best of both worlds. I'll be the fun aunt who gets to give the kids back at the end of the day or weekend."

Mac recalled the expression on Jessie's face earlier when she'd explained why having children was so important to her. He'd found himself buying into the fantasy right along with her until sanity returned and reminded him that he preferred the predictable. No unrealistic expectations, no naive belief that the people you loved would always be with you.

"Sounds like you've thought it through, but you're both still young. You might want to reconsider completely ruling out the idea of ever having children," the minister cautioned. "That said, we've saved the most interesting and challenging subjects for last, money and sex. These two issues can cause tons of stress in a marriage."

If Mac felt any more stress he'd explode. "Can we

wrap this up fairly quickly, Reverend?" Mac asked as he struggled to get air into his lungs. "We've agreed to keep our money separate and have no reason to doubt we're compatible." Mac glanced at his watch. "We need to get back to the office and work at clearing our desks or there won't be a honeymoon."

Reverend Miller smiled. "Well, you two seem to have thought everything out. I guess I'll see you Friday night then, at the museum, at five."

"Right." Mac shook the minister's hand. "And the DMA has an underground parking garage. If you park there, the elevator or stairs will take you to the entrance you need. On Saturday there will be valet parking."

"And the rehearsal dinner will be right after," Jessie added. "At La Grande Maison. Do you need directions?"

"I'm pretty familiar with downtown. It's obvious you two are ready to take this step. I'm looking forward to making your union official."

Mac couldn't get out of the minister's office quick enough. He needed air and distance from Jessie and the older man's wise, probing gaze.

"I'd say that went rather well, wouldn't you?" Jessie asked as they walked to his car.

Yeah, right. While meeting with the minister who was to marry him and Jenna, he'd been fantasizing about weekend getaways and being married to and having children with her sister.

Any jury in the world would find him guilty of being worse than scum. He should be hanged or shot, whichever proved more painful. "I'm just glad it's over. And your sister's little disappearing act had better be over, too. I'm calling her tonight and she'd better answer or call me back and actually speak to me."

"I don't blame you for being irritated with her, but it's no secret she can be self-absorbed. She just might not see the urgency in calling you back."

He shook his head. "I'll be very clear. And if you talk to her first, feel free to pass along the message that if she doesn't call tonight with news that she's on her way home, the wedding is off."

Mac sat at his desk, grateful for the quiet. The rest of the staff had left at five, which meant no interruptions for the past three hours.

Unfortunately, the lack of disturbances had failed to ensure focus, something he desperately needed since he'd fallen behind on his work because of all the unexpected wedding stuff.

No, that wasn't true. His problem with concentration centered solely on Jessie and his surprising, inappropriate reaction to her.

At lunch today, he'd been compelled to figure out why she was so set on having children of her own and why she resisted a career change.

Later on, during the interview, he'd been stunned by his own reaction to Jessie's suggestion of a weekend getaway to Hot Springs, after the minister had expressed the importance of setting aside time to spend as a couple.

Mac had been prepared to follow her anywhere, the excitement in her eyes a trait more seductive to him than stunning beauty or an hourglass figure.

He suspected the reason for his odd behavior had to

do with being thrown together with Jessie in somewhat intimate situations. Just the chance that it could be true scared the hell out of him and made no sense at all. Even if Jessie weren't his future sister-in-law, she still wouldn't be anyone he'd date, let alone want to marry. They had different goals, different views on family.

If Jenna had remained in town as planned, he wouldn't be dealing with *any* feelings for Jessie. No wonder, then, that out of frustration he'd come up with the ultimatum for his fiancée.

But he was well within his rights, dammit. It was countdown time, with only four days until the wedding.

His cell phone rang, as if on cue, and he checked the caller ID, relieved to see the number displayed belonged to Jenna. Finally, he could get some answers.

"Hi, Mac."

Mac hadn't needed caller ID to tell the twins apart. While Jenna spoke in a strong, direct manner, Jessie's voice possessed warmth with a calm self-assurance that he found intriguing and sexy as hell.

Big deal. So what if chemistry existed between him and Jessie? More was needed to make a partnership work.

"Hello, Jenna. Care to tell me what's really going on?"

"Didn't you get my message that everything was okay?"

"Let's just say I'm having a hard time buying that when you won't talk to me."

He heard a sigh. "Okay, you're right. There is something wrong, but it's not what you might think. I admit that the stress of planning the wedding got to me so I went out of town for a few days, but it wasn't long before my head cleared. I was all set to come home on Saturday when I had an allergic reaction to some makeup and my face was all swollen. So I tried a cream the pharmacist on the corner recommended and had an allergic reaction to *that*."

"But you're okay?"

"You mean aside from the fact my face is still swollen and the huge bags under my eyes make me look a hundred years old? It's horrible. No amount of makeup can hide this disaster."

He wasn't that big of a jerk that he'd kick someone when she was down. "Where are you? Maybe I can get the name of a specialist in the area."

"Thanks, but I think I've got it handled. I'm in Austin, at the spa, and they promise me that they'll have me back to my beautiful self by Friday."

"Friday? Isn't that cutting it pretty close?"

"Trust me, you wouldn't want to be seen with me the way I look right now. What's so urgent? I would've called sooner, but since I can't be seen in public, I've been pampering myself with massages and wraps. Before I could even check my messages, Jessie called and relayed your ultimatum."

"All hell has broken loose the past two days. Jessie and I had to deal with a surprise couples shower at the office and an interview with the minister. God knows what might be next, so I wanted you here."

"I'm sorry, but until the swelling goes down, there's nothing I can do."

"Then I'll cancel the walk-through with Craig on Thursday. The contract fell through that the other couple had on the house on Hillcrest that you were interested in. He's been promised first dibs on showing it again and was going to meet us there Thursday afternoon."

"That's wonderful! I know we only saw the house from the outside, but we went through a different house with the same floor plan, so other than maybe needing a few cosmetic changes, it's perfect for us. Can't you go without me?"

"No way. We'll just start house-hunting again when we get back from Hawaii."

"But someone else might snatch it up by then and I'm sure about the house," she insisted. "Can't you just make up some excuse for why I can't be there with you?"

"Craig knows you well enough by now that he'd never believe you'd go for the idea of me buying the house without you along." The last thing Mac needed was for his best man to suspect all wasn't well. Twice divorced, Craig was down on marriage to begin with. He'd probably try to talk Mac out of going through with the wedding.

"Then if all you need is me on your arm to close the deal, I'm sure Jessie will help out one more time."

"Jenna, this isn't fair to me or Jessie."

"You're right, but I promise to make it up to both of you when I get back. I've reconfirmed the wedding and reception arrangements by phone and I'm booked on the one o'clock flight out of Austin on Friday. I'll be back in plenty of time for the rehearsal dinner. I've talked to my parents and they know where I am. I've even convinced them to play nice at least until we get back from our honeymoon and they have a chance to really get to know you. So, you see, everything is under control. Trust me."

For some reason, Jenna's words, meant to reassure, filled Mac with a sense of foreboding. Too much had already gone wrong for him to feel optimistic about a problem-free finish.

Thursday afternoon, Mac stole a glance at Jessie before he made the turn into the cul-de-sac where the house was located that Jenna had shown interest in.

Jessie looked the part of her glamorous sister, but now that he'd spent time with her, he'd have no trouble telling them apart. She possessed a quiet confidence that hairstyle, makeup and clothes couldn't hide.

Thankfully, he'd had yesterday to regroup after having been so unnerved by the interview with the minister. And talking with Jenna had helped.

She had sounded like her old self, confident and, he had to admit, a little selfish. But, he could handle that as long as she took her position seriously as his partner at the firm once they returned from the honeymoon.

Still, he couldn't shake the premonition that things were going to get worse before they got better.

"Thanks again, Jessie, for doing us one more favor." He parked the car in front of the house, but kept it running for the air-conditioning while they waited on Craig. "I'm sure this wasn't how you planned to spend your vacation."

She chuckled. "That's an understatement. I never enjoyed pulling the twin switch when I was younger, although it did save my butt a few times, and I like it even less now."

"Then why do it?"

"She's my sister. She'd do the same for me. And besides, she had no way of knowing she'd have an allergic reaction to the makeup."

He had to admire Jessie's loyalty. "Whatever your reasons, I'm grateful." Although after the mega-stressful session with the minister, Mac had hoped that the next time he'd see her was at the rehearsal, with Jenn at his side. Once she returned, he'd be able to focus on what really mattered—the fact they shared common goals—and file away and forget the chemistry between him and Jessie.

"We'll see how grateful you are a few hours from now when we're back at my place and you're digging into what could only pass for dirt in Texas."

"I'll keep up my end of the deal," he promised, even though he had work piled up on his desk.

"If I had known about this ahead of time, I wouldn't have planned such a big project for this afternoon. It's supposed to rain later today and I'll be busy most of the weekend with the wedding, so there's no telling when I'd be able to get it all planted."

"You don't have to explain. I'm not an expert on landscaping, but even I know that with the June heat, the sooner you get the plants and shrubs into the ground, the better."

He could've offered to pay for someone to help her, but for one thing, he assumed she would refuse, and for another, he felt obligated to personally pay this debt. In his opinion, Jessie had gone above and beyond what the bond of sisterhood might require.

A red Mini Cooper pulled up ahead and parked along the curb. Craig exited the car with his briefcase and they joined him at the sidewalk.

Still the free spirit he'd been in college, Craig wore his blond hair a little longer than some might deem respectable and refused to wear a tie.

He admitted his appearance and atypical car scared away the more conservative potential clients, and didn't care, since he wouldn't want to work with that type anyway; the passion he brought to his work had made him one of the most successful Realtors in the area.

Craig kissed Jessie on the cheek. "You look great as always, Jenn," he said, then slapped Mac on the back. "Any chance I can change your mind about a bachelor party, buddy? It'd be tough to do this late, but I bet I could throw something together."

"Not a chance," Mac replied. "But thanks, anyway." He was already behind at the office, and he couldn't attack that workload until he'd toured the house and spent the rest of the afternoon digging.

Besides, the whole tradition seemed rather lame and juvenile.

"Let's get this show on the road, then." Craig punched in a code in the lockbox, opened the door and waved them inside. "I think this is exactly what you're looking for, except the master bath might be a deal-breaker. I think it has just a standard-size Jacuzzi tub."

Mac shrugged. "Depending on the layout, we might be able to move things around and replace it with an oversize one."

A puzzled expression appeared on Jessie's face.

"You won't mind a little remodeling, right, Jenn?" he asked, after he realized she probably knew her sister preferred showers to baths. He and Jenn had already had this conversation with Craig on earlier house-hunting trips.

"No. Of course not."

Craig grinned. "I still say real men don't take bubble baths."

"Hey, I don't use the sweet-smelling stuff," Mac protested. "It's therapeutic, that's all. Started taking them after I hurt my knee in college." So what if he took baths now to relax?

"Yeah, and it was embarrassing as all get out."

Mac glanced at Jessie, only to discover a wicked gleam in her eyes. She leaned into him and tugged at his tie. "I don't know, Craig. I think real women go for a man who isn't afraid of bubbles."

Chapter Seven

Mac swallowed hard. He'd never imagined house-hunting could be anything but a harmless outing, never dreamed Jessie would play along with him, enjoy his discomfort when he couldn't do a thing about it.

Jessie wouldn't, and he was an idiot. For a minute he'd forgotten she was playing a role. Jenna could flirt and tease with the best of them. Jessie wasn't like that—or was she?

No, he refused to go there, didn't want to know if she could act the playful seductress.

An unfamiliar ring filled the room, thank God, and Craig checked the caller ID on his cell phone. "I need to take this call. Take a look around and I'll catch up."

"No problem." Mac forced himself to place his hand on the small of Jessie's back as they walked down the hall to the kitchen. He'd already been caught once for acting out of character and Craig knew him even better than his staff. "Remember, Jenna's main concern is if the floor plan is suitable for entertaining," he whispered. "So keep that in mind as you look."

Jessie nodded absently as she ran her hand along the countertop and frowned, all traces of the teasing vixen gone. "This solid beige will show every little mark or stain. And hardwood floors are really high maintenance."

"Not an issue. We'll have hired help."

Jessie opened the French doors and stepped outside onto the patio and shook her head. "The pool takes up the whole backyard."

"So?"

"There wouldn't be any room for a dog to play, let alone kids."

"Since we don't intend to have either one, that's not an issue."

A strange look appeared on her face. "Oh, right. Well, it's a great pool for swimming laps. You could even put up a volleyball net at the shallow end. Jenna would love that."

Jessie walked over to the family room, which boasted vaulted ceilings, a wet bar and fireplace.

"This is perfect for entertaining," he said, confident she couldn't find fault with the expansive room.

"But won't you feel lost in it when it's just the two of you?"

The thought had never crossed his mind. "Let's check out the guest rooms downstairs before we go up."

"You mean the master is upstairs?"

"Yes. Why?"

She shook her head. "Never mind."

"What?"

"I keep forgetting this isn't about what kind of house *I* would want," she said softly, obviously worried about Craig overhearing.

"And what might that be?" Mac found himself asking, even though it shouldn't matter.

"I'd want a big backyard with a swing set, sandbox and doghouse." A dreamy smile appeared on her face. "The countertops should have a busy pattern in it so spills and stains aren't a big deal. While the kids are little, I'd use the guest rooms downstairs as nurseries, so I'd definitely want the master downstairs so I could be close by. But once they're older, they can move upstairs so mom and dad can have privacy."

"How many?"

"How many what?"

"Dogs. Kids. How many do you want?"

"Oh, one dog to start with. At least two children, maybe more." She pointed to the ground. "So this cream carpet would be a nightmare. There wouldn't be a white wall in the house. I'd want warm colors that made the room welcoming. And although it's nice to have lots of space, I'd want the rooms a little smaller so it would feel more cozy."

As Mac listened to her describe her imaginary, close-knit family and dream home, he was filled with an aching need that made it hard to breathe.

Childhood memories flooded his mind, reminding him of how his mother had made their small house a home for him and his brother, how she made the simple things seem special.

But after his brother's death, the joy had disappeared from his mother's eyes. He had vowed then to never have children; he didn't want to ever experience the pain of losing a child.

Back then, he'd been helpless to diminish his mother's grief, but through his work now he could at least bring to justice those in the medical and insurance professions who were incompetent and caused others so much suffering.

Jessie's dream involved too many risks, yet a part of him wished it were possible for him to take that leap of faith.

What the hell was he thinking? He needed out of the house, away from Jessie and her fantasies that had nothing to do with real life.

"Sorry it took so long," Craig offered as he entered the family room. "Are you ready to check out the upstairs?"

Mac was ready, all right. Ready for his life to get back to normal. Except that wouldn't happen until his fiancée returned home.

Once Jenna was by his side, her bold and sassy ways would quickly remind him of why they belonged together. "We've seen enough. You know what our bottom line is, so draw up the papers and fax them over to me later."

Craig raised his eyebrows. "You're telling me that you want to make an offer without seeing the upstairs? That's not like you, Mac."

Mac grabbed Jessie's hand and headed for the front door. "No, but it is like Jenna," he called out over his shoulder. "She knows what she wants. Thanks, man, and

I'll see you tomorrow at the DMA for the rehearsal, five sharp."

He closed the door behind him and used his remote to unlock his car. Now he could breathe.

Jessie directed Mac to the guest bathroom where he could change into "working" clothes, then hurried to her bedroom to do the same.

Swapping her sophisticated pantsuit for a pair of denim shorts and T-shirt, she then pulled her hair back into a ponytail and scoured her closet for an old pair of tennis shoes.

What in the world was going on with Mac? All the way home, he had refused to level with her about what had prompted such an abrupt exit, which had left his friend perplexed, to say the least.

Craig might be the more laid-back of the two men, but he wasn't stupid. She had immediately liked the shaggy-haired maverick with a trace of sadness in his eyes.

Heck, the reason she'd agreed to the charade in the first place was to keep the best man in the dark about Jenna's absence, only to have Mac yank her away in the midst of a conversation without letting her say a proper goodbye. Again.

The man needed to work on his exits. "So much for not arousing any suspicion," she muttered under her breath.

She came out of her bedroom to find him staring out her kitchen patio. He had changed into a T-shirt and shorts that revealed muscular arms and powerful looking legs; his hands rested on lean hips. Lord, but he looked more tempting than the richest chocolate.

Her mouth grew dry, her throat tight.

So what if he was a hunk? She had no business reacting to him as if he were just any sexy man standing in her kitchen. He was her future brother-in-law.

He was also a meddler who refused to understand her need to approach a career change cautiously, although she had to admit that his solution of working with kids outside of school held a certain appeal.

In fact, she'd made an appointment to talk to her principal tomorrow morning about the pros and cons of the job. But she was only on a mission to gather facts at this point.

At the moment, though, she needed to deal with Mac. It was safer to stir things up than fixate on a temptation that could do more harm to her heart than a calorie-laden box of chocolates could do to her thighs. "Look, Mac, you've made it clear that you don't want to talk about what happened back at the cold-stone mansion, but I have to know. Is it because I sort of blew it as far as pretending to like what my sister does? Were you afraid I'd let something slip in front of Craig?"

Mac turned around, his face void of expression. "It hardly matters now."

"But the whole point of my coming with you was to keep your friend from thinking anything was wrong. The way you so rudely dragged me out of there, he's bound to wonder what's going on."

"Craig's so busy salivating over the big commission he'll make that I doubt he noticed anything." Mac stuffed his hands into the pockets of his shorts. "I already know Jenna will love the house, so there wasn't any reason to waste more time."

"But—"

He nodded in the direction of her backyard. "It looks like it could start raining any minute. We'll be lucky to finish planting before it hits. Shouldn't we get started?"

She gave up, and added obstinate to brooding and rude on Mac's list of irksome traits.

Two hours later, Jessie had to admit that the quality she'd found irritating earlier, she now saw as an asset. The man was tenacious; he only stopped to wipe sweat from his forehead.

Ice-cold water from the cooler on her porch helped to take the edge off the almost unbearable heat. She wouldn't have blamed Mac if he'd removed his shirt, but was thankful he hadn't.

The more of Mac's body that remained covered the better. She had found it increasingly difficult to keep her mind on landscaping and off how she imagined he'd look stripped of his clothes and in *her* oversize tub. She had bubble bath, and more, she'd gladly share.

A bead of sweat dropped into her eye, pulling her out of her fantasy. Oh, Lord, she was losing it. Too long in the sun. Too much exposure to a man wrong for her in too many ways to count.

And at the moment, the said Mr. Wrong had grabbed the wrong plant. "Wait, Mac," Jessie called out. "The other bush goes in that corner."

"What difference does it make? They're about the same size. They're both green."

She shook her head. So clueless. "One needs morning sun, the other needs mostly shade."

He swapped bushes, then strode to the hole he had dug at the southeast corner of her backyard. "What did you do, spend a week in a library researching all this?" His shoulder and back muscles bunched and strained as he maneuvered the bush into the hole.

Knock it off, Jessie. "You make it sound like a chore, but I've always loved plants and most things that grow."

She grabbed a flat of English ivy and carried it over to the pink crepe myrtle. A blanket of green underneath would provide the perfect anchoring effect for a tree that bloomed so pretty and so heavy. "While I'm having coffee and bird-watching, I scour magazines for ideas, then read up on the specific plants to make sure they grow in this region and what the requirements are."

"How do you find the time? Don't teachers have to bring work home a lot, grade papers, plan lessons?"

"You make time for something you enjoy." She wasn't about to admit that she had never intended to work on her backyard before the wedding. But she had needed a guaranteed distraction that would keep her too busy to think about, let alone fantasize about, a man completely off-limits.

Boy, had that plan backfired.

Jessie dug another hole, inserted one of the ivy plants and covered the roots with new, enriched soil. Too bad guilt wasn't a fertilizer, since she had plenty to spare.

Because although Jenna was at fault for the stressful events of the past week, at the moment Jessie had no one to blame but herself for blatantly lusting over her sister's fiancé.

So what was she supposed to do with all the guilt? Bury it like some guilty treasure?

She'd need a bigger backyard.

The sky grew overcast, offering welcome relief from the relentless sun.

"We'd better hurry," Mac offered as he gazed at the sky. "Those rain clouds are moving in pretty fast."

"I'm done here." She stood and brushed the dirt from her knees. "There's just the one tree and a couple of flats of flowers for pots. I can do those later."

She helped him dig the last hole for the small tree she hoped at some point would offer additional shade for her patio.

Why did it feel so wonderful to have someone working side by side with her? Normally, she gardened alone and enjoyed the solitude.

Who was she kidding? Just anyone wouldn't have doubled her enjoyment of bringing her backyard to life with color and texture. Only Mac.

The undeniable fact that nothing could come of her feelings for him filled her with a deep sense of disappointment and regret. At most, they could be friends, but her body and heart seemed determined to ignore the message.

Time and enough Sunday family dinners and holidays spent in the midst of the happily married couple would no doubt cure that problem. She'd become an expert in hiding how she really felt about Mac.

For now, though, she'd enjoy this last afternoon together, then she'd cut off her feelings at the roots to ensure they couldn't grow back.

Mac twisted the slender tree trunk and rocked it into place inside the hole. "I can handle it from here, Jess," he insisted.

He smothered a groan when Jessie ignored him, knelt down and put her small hands beneath his, her mouth temptingly close. "No, I want to help."

Too bad he couldn't tell her that the best way she could help was to take her cute butt inside. All afternoon her presence had been pure distraction in the secluded backyard.

She had impressed him with her vast knowledge of plants and their care. Even more beautiful with her hair in a ponytail and dressed in old clothes, she was also unpretentious and quick to laugh at herself.

To his surprise, he had enjoyed toiling in the yard, although he'd grumbled occasionally to hide the fact. But he refused to admit his pleasure had anything to do with Jessie's presence. He'd simply forgotten how rewarding it was to work with his hands, or so he tried to convince himself.

The rain changed from light sprinkles to a soft, steady shower as they loosely packed enriched soil around the trunk, then scoured the yard for shovels and empty containers.

He couldn't keep his eyes off Jessie. The rain had plastered her shirt and jean shorts against her skin, outlining in great detail each enticing curve.

God, but she was beautiful. And out of bounds. So why couldn't he rein in the attraction he felt for her? And why didn't he feel the same lust for Jenna, who looked so much like Jessie?

Until this week, he'd been in control of all aspects of his life. Although he might not be able to promise a winning verdict for a client, he could guarantee he'd given his all to the case. At least that claim would've been valid six days ago, when he could still focus.

He'd intentionally chosen a woman to marry who agreed with him that love was an unnecessary distraction, only to find his life intertwined with a woman who couldn't be more wrong for him. Yet on more than one occasion, he'd found himself being pulled into her fantasy that involved love, marriage, kids and even a dog.

And he had no doubt she'd be a great mother because of her gentleness, creativity and patience, the same traits that made her an excellent teacher and gardener.

Laughter skipped across the raindrops. "I know I probably look like a drowned rat," Jessie said with a grin. "But you're a drowned, *dirty* rat."

"That just means I worked harder."

She rolled her eyes. "So, Mac, what do you think your clients would say if they could see you now?"

For the second time that day he chose to believe she was innocently teasing him, but there was nothing innocent about his response.

The invisible shield he'd thrown up to help him remain detached the moment he realized Jessie's effect on him obviously needed improvements, because it did nothing to dull his senses.

He'd severely underestimated the power of the playfulness in her voice, the smell of her subtle yet sexy perfume. She stood less than a foot away; he could look to his heart's content, but never possess what he wanted most.

In danger of exploding from all of his pent-up energy, he grasped at the first idea that popped into his head. *Nothing wrong with a good, clean mud fight.* He kicked mud on her soaked shoes.

"Hey, cut it out."

"What do you think your students would say if they could see *you?*" He flicked wet dirt on her shirt.

Her eyes grew wide, her mouth gaped. "Okay, this means war." She bent down, scooped up mud from an empty juniper container, then tossed the gooey contents at his knees.

He glanced around the yard, noticed the wheelbarrow half-full of the clay-like dirt from the various holes they'd dug. Before she could react, he lunged forward, picked her up and threw her over his shoulder.

She shrieked and pounded harmlessly against his back with her fists. "Let me down!"

"Be glad to." He deposited her in the wheelbarrow, then crossed his arms in front of him to admire his handiwork.

Her face scrunched up, her eyes sparked with fire. "You're dead meat, now, McKenna," she threatened, then struggled to get out. But between her wet clothes and the soft, sticky mud, she couldn't.

She started giggling. Her shoulders shook and she held her stomach as the giggle turned to full-blown laughter. God, he loved how she enjoyed life, how quick she was to find the humor in a situation.

His laughter joined hers as he scooped her out of the wheelbarrow. Suddenly, she grew still in his arms. He made the mistake of meeting her gaze and discovered a longing that took him by surprise and filled him with mind-numbing anticipation.

The playful mood evaporated quicker than dew on a Texas summer morning. The intoxicating sensation of her warm body pressed against him melted his resistance.

Her mouth hovered mere inches from his. The gnawing need to taste those tempting lips pushed away any reminders of why it was wrong to want her. He devoured her mouth, expecting to find the sweet innocence he'd experienced during their earlier, brief kiss, but instead she fed him hungry, life-sustaining kisses that only made him want more.

He loosened his grip, allowing her legs to lower to the ground, then urgently pressed the length of her body against his.

She moaned and drew closer as if she, too, couldn't bear any space between them. The taste of her mouth and the feel of her responsive body against his made him crazy with need. He'd never wanted a woman more.

What had ever made him think his perfect mate should be glamorous and driven? He held perfection in his arms, a woman who was down-to-earth and intent on stopping to smell the roses she had just planted.

Jessie had thought that nothing could rival the effect Mac's cologne had on her hormones, but now she knew better. He smelled of fresh air and sweat and his greedy kisses threatened to send her over the edge.

Rain continued to fall, rinsing away the dirt on her clothes and the common sense and willpower she had relied on for the past week. Now, she simply prayed that Mac would never stop kissing her, touching her.

She would have been able to fight a simple case of lust, but circumstances had forced her to know *all* of him: the man who worked tirelessly for his clients, who treated his staff like family, who was convinced he didn't want love because of a tragedy in his past.

Yet, the emotion in that same man's gaze and the tenderness of his surprisingly unsteady hands told a different story.

Lord help her, but she'd fallen in love with her soon-to-be brother-in-law.

Thunder rumbled in the sky and cruelly jerked her out of the sensual fog.

Mac jumped back as if struck by the lightning that had no doubt preceded the clap of thunder, when they'd been too lost in each other to notice. "I'd be lying if I said I was sorry this happened," Mac said, his voice low and husky. "So I'm just going to promise it won't happen again. It can't."

"I know. I'm not sorry, either, but I agree it was a mistake." She knew from her work in the garden the importance of timing. If a seed was planted too early or too late in the season, it would lie dormant in the ground, unable to break through to the open air and sunshine.

Her feelings for Mac had surfaced too late. They shouldn't have surfaced at all....

"Don't worry. It's already forgotten," she assured, even though she knew a part of her would never forget how his kisses had touched her very soul, how his faith in her abilities had challenged her to examine what she really wanted for the future and to go after it, instead of holding back.

She loved him, but he was obviously still committed to going through with the wedding to her sister.

His intention to do the right thing only made Jessie love him more.

Mac heard the front door open, then smelled burgers and fries. But he hadn't ordered anything delivered to the office.

"Is my boy working too hard, as usual?"

"Mom?"

He met his mother in his doorway and enveloped her in a hug. "What are you doing here, besides feeding a starving man?"

"I left Houston earlier than I'd planned. When you didn't answer at the condo, I assumed, correctly I might add, that you were here and probably hadn't eaten dinner and it's already seven."

"You know me too well." Except that he didn't have much of an appetite. What had he been thinking when he'd gone against all logic and common sense and kissed Jessie?

He never should have given in to the chemistry. Even if he weren't engaged to her sister, Jessie was all wrong for him. He couldn't be the kind of man Jessie wanted— a man who would turn his back on his life's mission, a man who could become a father and take the risk of losing his child.

After he'd left Jessie's, he'd showered and changed into dry clothes and returned to his office. He had taken refuge in the work that had piled up while he'd been busy trying to fool everyone that all was well with him and his fiancée.

"Mac, what's wrong?"

The sound of his mother's voice snapped him back to the present. "What? I mean, nothing is wrong." He pointed at the sack of food. "You're joining me, right?"

"Of course." She set the bag on his desk and frowned. "But don't try and change the subject. Tell me what's bothering you."

He massaged his right temple. "It's just pre-wedding jitters. No big deal. It happens to everyone, right?"

"Like you said, I know you too well." She folded her hands across her chest. "I'm not buying it. Try again."

Since a full confession wasn't an option, he decided on half-truths. "All right. I'm a little uptight because Jenna unexpectedly left town and has been gone all week."

"That doesn't make any sense. Have you spoken with her?"

"Finally. She's in Austin. It's a long story, but she has a good reason for not coming back to town right away. Still, even though she's assured me that she hasn't changed her mind about getting married, I suspect part of the reason she's stayed away so long is cold feet."

His mother began to pull sandwiches out of the bag. "I'm sure everything will work out. You sound perfect for each other and, trust me, love will see you and Jenna through a case of cold feet and more during your long and happy married life."

He didn't bother to reveal love wasn't the foundation

of their marriage because his mother would never understand. Even worse, after what happened with Jessie, he wasn't sure he did.

Mac glanced at his watch and decided to call it a day, or night, more to the point. Nine o'clock. And he still had at least a full day's work he needed to finish before he left town on Saturday.

His mother had left for her hotel soon after they'd eaten. He always invited her to stay with him, since he had an extra room, but she insisted a grown man needed his privacy. He imagined it was the other way around, though. She'd never remarried after divorcing his father over twenty years ago and was pretty set in her ways.

He heard the front door open and frowned. Who would come by so late?

"Anybody need a drink around here?"

Mac groaned. "Come on in, Craig." First his mother and now his best friend. Who was next, Reverend Miller? "But it'll have to be quick, buddy."

Craig sauntered into the office with a bottle of champagne in one hand and two glasses in the other. "Surely you have time for a pre-wedding toast."

"Of course."

"Since you nixed the bachelor party idea, I figured this was the least I could do."

"It wasn't necessary, but thanks."

Craig poured the bubbly into the glasses, handed one to Mac, then picked up the other one and raised it in the air.

"To the best friend a guy could have."

Mac raised his then took a drink. "Nice toast, but a little mushy for you, isn't it?"

"So, sue me. It's my first shot at being best man. That's why I've been on the fence about whether I should say anything."

"About?"

"You were there for me during some bad times, and I want to be as good of a friend to you."

"Craig, where is this going?" he asked, but suspected he knew the answer.

"This afternoon both you and Jenna were acting strange. Are you two fighting?"

Mac shook his head. "Just the usual pre-wedding jitters."

"So you aren't having second thoughts about the marriage? Because if you are, it's never too late to call the wedding off. Even though you'd hate to hurt or embarrass Jenna, it's better to act honestly now. Believe me, if you wait, it causes even more pain later when the inevitable breakup happens."

Craig set his glass down on the desk. "There. I said it. So, tell me the truth, do you still think getting married is the right thing to do?"

"Absolutely," Mac insisted, although he wondered who he was trying to convince more, his buddy or himself.

Chapter Eight

Jessie pulled into her driveway late Friday morning and groaned at the sight of her friends on her front porch. She knew she could tell them anything and they'd be supportive, but she still felt raw from what had happened between her and Mac the day before. She wasn't sure she wanted them to know about her terrible lapse in judgment regarding her sister's fiancé.

"Hey, Jess," Carla called out. "You were out early today. Doctor appointment or something?"

Jessie decided she might as well confess. They'd get it out of her sooner or later. "Actually, I met with Mrs. Drew."

"Our boss?" Dana asked. "No one got fired did they?"

"Nothing like that." Although Jessie was still reeling from the realization she loved the one man she could never have, she had decided to keep the meeting with her boss for that very reason—a major change in her life might make things easier once Jenna and Mac returned from their honeymoon and got on with their lives as a married couple.

"Is something else wrong, then?" Dana pressed.

At least discussing her career would offer a distraction. What happened yesterday with Mac wouldn't even have to come up. "Come on inside," Jessie offered and opened the front door. "And I'll fill you in."

Jessie led the way to the kitchen where they settled in their usual seats around the table. "Nothing is wrong, in fact, it's good news. I'm finally ready to leave third grade and get certified to become a principal, so I met with Mrs. Drew to get more information."

"Are you sure?" Dana asked. "You won't find a better school than ours."

Carla elbowed Dana. "This is about what Jessie needs. She'll make a great principal."

Dana rubbed her arm. "Of course you will, Jess. I know I'm being selfish. I'll miss not having my best friend right down the hall. But you've talked about this a long time, and it's obviously something you want, so you *should* go after it."

Jessie nodded, grateful for her friend's support. "While I was talking to Mrs. Drew this morning, it dawned on me that was exactly why I had put off taking the next step. She's created this warm, accepting environment, made us all feel like family, which is very important to me and I didn't want to give it up."

"So what changed your mind?" Carla asked.

Aside from hoping a career change would help fill a void in her life, now that she'd fallen in love with the one man she couldn't have? "Mrs. Drew told me that if I wanted to remain at her school as a third grade teacher because it's what I felt called to do, she would fight to keep me on her staff. I admitted that while I've loved teaching, I'm ready for another challenge. I want to effect change from the top down. As a principal, I'd teach teachers, so I'd be able to help even more kids. And I'd shamelessly follow Mrs. Drew's example. Whatever school district hires me, I'll treat the staff of the school they assign me to like family, and I'll look out for the interest of each student."

"But won't you miss having your own students?" Dana asked. Only a fellow teacher could understood the bond between teachers and their students.

"I'm sure I will to a point, but I also think I'll love the challenge of taking a poor or mediocre school and making it great. Let's face it, not all schools are lucky enough to have a leader like Mrs. Drew. And I can still come visit all of you when I get homesick."

Carla put her hand on Jessie's arm. "Well, I think it's a great idea. What's the next step?"

"I'll need to go back to school and get a mid-management certification, then work as an assistant principal for a while. So this will be my last year teaching."

Jessie couldn't believe how good it felt to actually say out loud that she was following her dream. If only her personal life wasn't such a mess. "So, now you know why I was up early. What got you up and around before noon, Dana? Our nail appointments aren't until one."

"Oh, um, Carla thought it'd be fun to make a whole day of it and go to lunch, maybe shop."

Jessie suspected something was up. Dana hated mornings almost as much as she dreaded shopping. She'd only gone along with the manicures to appease them. "Okay, what's really going on? Why were you two camped out on my door this morning?"

"We're worried about you," Dana blurted. "We know about Mac."

Jessie felt the color drain from her face. "What do you mean?"

"I wasn't spying, I swear." Carla squeezed Jessie's arm. "You had said you were planning on working in your yard all day yesterday. I'd been stuck inside painting the bathroom and needed a break, so when it started to rain I peeked over the fence to see if you wanted help and saw you and Mac, you know, kissing."

Dana put a hand on Jessie's other arm. "We're not judging you, Jess. We just want to know that you're okay."

Jessie *could not* show her panic. She had to downplay what had happened between her and Mac precisely because nothing would ever come of it. She bought a little time by reaching for her much-needed antacids.

She could barely admit to herself she loved him; no one else needed to know, she told herself as she popped two tablets into her mouth.

Carla nodded. "When I checked later, his car was gone and you didn't answer your phone, so I thought, well, that you might have left with him. Which wouldn't be like you at all, and I didn't know what to do so I called Dana over this morning."

"Mac went home alone, I went to bed early." The truth. "So you've been worried over nothing." A lie.

Her stomach churned under the stress of pretending, from living a lie in some shape or form all week long.

"But what about the kiss," Carla persisted. "I didn't imagine it. There was *steam* coming off you two."

"The kiss took us both by surprise." The truth. "It's been pretty stressful with me filling in for Jenna all week, so we were kidding around, having a mud fight in the rain, and then things got out of hand and the kiss just sort of happened."

"I can see how it would get confusing," Dana offered. "You and Jenna look so much alike. And Mac is easy on the eyes. You could forget who you were, who he is."

Jessie nodded, although she knew there were no excuses. "We both feel terrible about it, but the important thing is that we agree it was a mistake and will never happen again."

Carla let out a sigh and sat back in her chair. "What a relief. Deep down I knew you wouldn't *really* fool around with your sister's fiancé, but after seeing that kiss, my imagination just took off. I'm sorry."

"You have nothing to apologize for. So, someone mentioned lunch. Where and when?"

Jessie half listened as her friends threw out suggestions for restaurants. At first she'd been less than thrilled to see them on her doorstep, and filled with dread when they confessed the real reason for their visit, but now she was grateful.

She'd keep busy all afternoon, and once she saw her sister on Mac's arm at the rehearsal, putting Jenna's happiness first would be an easy choice.

Well, maybe not easy, but certainly the right choice.

* * *

Mac kept an eye out for Jessie while he listened to the wedding coordinator introduce herself. "So what do you think, Mr. McKenna?" Whitney, a tall brunette, pointed at the glass flower sculptures attached to a wide expanse of windows in the atrium of the Dallas Museum of Art. The large open area would be used for the reception. "You won't find this backdrop in many wedding albums."

"I'm sure that's why Jenna picked the DMA over the other sites she mentioned." When Jenna had warned him that the ordinary wouldn't do for the high-profile wedding she had planned, he'd offered no objections. She didn't know the meaning of subtle, but she always showed class.

"We'll remove everything but the tables and chairs from the atrium, which will look romantic and elegant for the reception by the time we're done decorating. We'll bring in our own lighting, since candles can't be used on the premises. For the wedding, chairs will be set up in the corridor here, with an aisle in between. The maid of honor and the bride will come down the stairs at the other end and meet you, your best man and the minister at this end. It makes for a very dramatic entrance."

"Mac, are you sure Jenna is on her way?" Reverend Miller asked after another glance at his watch.

"I'm sure." Mac wondered if they were all going to hell for lying to a minister. "Just give her five more minutes."

Jessie, playing the part of the bride-to-be yet again because of a last-minute flight cancellation, had purposely arranged to arrive late in order to bypass formal introductions and the usual small talk.

The less interaction between Jessie and his mother, best man and the minister, the better. And although her parents knew about the twin switch, he worried they might accidentally reveal the truth and ruin the entire evening.

But if all went as planned, the sisters would swap clothes at the restaurant before the rehearsal dinner and no one would be the wiser.

The door to the stairway of the DMA's underground parking garage opened and Jessie appeared, her cheeks flushed, her manner flustered as she hurried toward the museum entrance and dashed inside.

Her "kiss me" red dress had a slit to one side that revealed a glimpse of her shapely legs with each step. She took his breath away and he reveled in the fact he didn't have to hide it, since she was his fiancée, after all.

"I'm so sorry, everyone," she said breathlessly and gave him a quick peck on his right cheek.

His mother appeared by his side and he introduced them, which ended in a hug.

"We'd better get started," Whitney urged.

"I understand your maid of honor can't make it tonight, Jenna," Reverend Miller said with a frown. "You'll need to fill her in."

"She's sorry, but it couldn't be helped. I'll tell her what she needs to know for tomorrow." Jessie turned to her father, who had appeared by her side. "I believe we come down the stairs and walk down the corridor to here, right, Whitney?"

"Right."

Jessie, who had obviously been prepped by her sister, headed for the stairway with her father. The coordinator turned to Craig. "You will seat the bride's mother in the front row on her side, then the groom will seat his on the other, and you'll both join the reverend here, in the center. So, let's run through it real quick, okay?"

Mac and the others nodded. The sooner he could get the rehearsal over and get to the restaurant for the dinner, the better. Seeing Jenna again would clear his head and get his mind back on reality and the future he really wanted.

Within minutes he was escorting his mother down the corridor. The limestone pavement, raised in some places and level in others, added dimension while the wide hallway's lower ceiling created a sense of intimacy in the midst of the huge, grand building.

"This is all so rushed, Mac," his mother whispered. "There wasn't even time for me to chat with Jenna."

He patted his mother's arm. "I know, but we'll make up for it at dinner. I'll make sure you're sitting next to each other."

"I'm looking forward to it. And I already know I like her because it's obvious how much you love each other."

Great. First he'd acted as an accessory in deceiving a minister and now his mother. Mac knew for sure he was going to hell now.

Jessie and her father made their entrance; he delivered her to Mac, then joined her mother. Jessie faced Mac, and as if to gather strength from each other, they instinctively reached for one another's hands while the minister performed an abbreviated version of their vows.

As Mac stared into her shimmering green eyes, a crazy part of him wished that the rehearsal was the real ceremony. He swore he saw the same yearning in Jessie's gaze, but convinced himself that he had imagined it because nothing could change the fact that he couldn't give her the life she dreamed of.

"Mr. McKenna?"

Mac shook his head to clear the unwanted, illogical, unsettling thoughts. "Sorry. What did you say, Whitney?"

"Just that at the end, after the reverend presents you as husband and wife, you'll turn around and face your guests, they'll clap, of course, and then you'll proceed down the aisle toward the back. Everyone will gather there for champagne and canapés while we move the chairs into the atrium and finish setting up for the reception."

Mac nodded. "Right." He glanced at his watch as an excuse to avoid Jessie's gaze. "I guess we can head over to La Grande Maison for the rehearsal dinner, then."

At least he'd have solitude for the ride to the restaurant since everyone had driven their own cars downtown. He'd use that time to regroup and forget about emotion in favor of logic.

What was the point in fantasizing about a life he didn't want, with a woman he would only end up hurting in the end because of their conflicting priorities?

Jenna was perfect for him. Once he saw her again, his doubts would disappear.

Jessie gripped the marble counter of La Grand Maison's elegant bathroom and prayed she wouldn't throw up.

Damn her nervous stomach. Guilt did it to her every

time. She should have fought harder against the attraction she felt for Mac, should never have given in to the temptation to kiss that gorgeous mouth.

But she'd been taken by surprise yesterday and her guard had been down. One minute, they'd been laughing and throwing mud, and the next...

No excuses. Some things a person just didn't do. Lusting after and kissing your sister's fiancé had to rank high on that list.

The fact that Jessie now knew she loved him was, and would remain, irrelevant. She had deserved to feel the gut-wrenching pain earlier as she pretended to be Mac's fiancée during the rehearsal. Deserved to be bent over now and half-sick from such disloyalty to her sister.

The rest room door opened, followed by the scent of a familiar perfume.

"Jess, what's wrong?"

Tears formed in Jessie's eyes at the sound of her sister's voice, but she was too shaken to speak.

Jenna appeared at her side. "You look awful. Are you sick?"

"I'll be fine," Jessie assured, then glanced up. "You look great and so...serene. How, with things such a mess?"

"Au contraire, sis. Things couldn't be better. The people at the spa took great care of me, so I'm good as new. And thanks to you, the rehearsal went on as planned. If you hadn't filled in for me at the rehearsal, we would've lost our reservations for the dinner here, and I wanted everything perfect for Mac. I owe him that."

Jessie still had no idea how she'd managed to act so normal and calm at the rehearsal. Compared to that, a gourmet meal at a five-star restaurant should go down as easy as their best wine.

"And I do thank you, Jess. You've never cared for deception, so the entire past week and the rehearsal tonight must've been tough on you."

Amen, Jessie thought. But refusing to participate in the charade one last time tonight hadn't been an option. She was too immersed in the tangled web to back out at the last minute and ruin her sister's chance with the man and the life she claimed she wanted.

"But so many things already went wrong today," Jessie said, having had most of the day to imagine many of the possibilities in her own mind. "Your flight was canceled and all the others were booked. What if you'd had trouble with the car you rented and couldn't get to the dinner on time? What if I *had* cracked under the pressure of pretending to be you in front of the minister, the best man and Mac's mother?"

"Relax and take some deep breaths." Jenna grabbed a paper towel and dabbed at the sweat on Jessie's face. "Thank goodness I thought to bring my makeup bag in." She glanced at Jessie's ears and frowned. "What made you pick *those* earrings to wear with that outfit? The hoops go better."

"That's the least of our problems." Jessie attempted to stand up straight. She still felt queasy, but the extra antacids she'd popped on the way over had begun to take the edge off. "Pick a stall. We need to swap clothes."

She hurried inside the closest one. As she undressed

she draped each piece across the top of the adjoining wall while Jenna did the same.

Just one more day. Jessie prayed for the strength to keep from losing her composure for another twenty-four hours. After the wedding, the happy couple would leave on their honeymoon.

Jenna would be the woman by Mac's side on the white beaches of Maui. She'd be the one receiving his scorching kisses, sharing his bed, his hopes, his dreams.

Stop it, Jessie. No sense in torturing herself. She'd use the time the newlyweds were out of town to box up her feelings for Mac and store them in some far recess of her mind.

She'd be like those people who were incapable of throwing away things they had no use for; the objects would be tucked away in an attic, destined to never see the light of day again. Yes, she'd keep her wrong, forbidden feelings out of sight, but forgetting the love she had for Mac and how he made her feel wasn't an option.

Too bad she couldn't find comfort in the fact that the love was one-sided and never meant to be because they wanted different things out of life.

Several minutes later, she put on the heels that had been scooted under the stall and joined her sister at the long vanity.

"Quick, give me the hair clip, Jess."

Jessie removed the clip from her hair and let it fall loosely to her shoulders. Jenna then put her hair up in the same style Jessie had worn earlier.

Jenna frowned and pushed her cosmetics case across the counter. "You're still white as a sheet."

Jessie reapplied makeup, but in her own light-handed manner, then they swapped jewelry.

"Why didn't you wear the shoes that match this dress?"

Jessie bit her tongue to keep from saying something flippant. No matter how annoying her sister could behave, at least she'd never been disloyal. "I did the best I could, Jenn."

Jenna smiled. "That's okay. Only Mom will notice, and she knows what's going on."

"Which reminds me, what reason do I give for missing the rehearsal?"

"Oh, what about some homeowner thing? The washing machine flooded, or something? I don't think anyone will make a big deal out of it."

Another lie, but at least a harmless one. Jessie was amazed by how Jenna, who usually fed on drama and intrigue, seemed to be taking everything in stride.

Jessie studied her sister. "I still can't get over how good you look. Did you really have an allergic reaction or just cold feet?"

Jenna shuddered. "Trust me, it was horrible."

"But how can you be so calm? If it was the night before my wedding, I think I'd be a nervous wreck."

"I'm just so relieved the swelling went down in time. And I'm sure all the wraps and massages at the spa didn't hurt. But I think the main reason is because now I'm really sure that this is what I want. I admit that seeing Dylan again made me doubt myself for a while, but at the same time, those few days spent around him made me realize chemistry alone isn't enough. Dylan had no interest in my work and would've been content to let me support us as he followed *his* dream."

Jenna smiled and clasped Jessie's hands in hers. "Mac and I make a great team. We're compatible, we want the same things out of life. Our life together is going to be great, I know it."

Still no mention of love.

Jessie had no doubt her love for Mac was real, but even if he felt the same, she could never put her own happiness above her sister's. Betrayal wasn't an option, even as she felt pain in both her stomach and her heart. "I wish you the best, Jenn. I hope you and Mac are very happy together."

La Grande Maison might as well have been a hole-in-the-wall diner instead of a five-star restaurant for all the attention Mac had given the place since he'd arrived with the wedding party.

He only had eyes for the woman across from him, and unfortunately, she wasn't his bride-to-be. But he couldn't seem to stop himself from stealing glances at Jessie as he forced down what was probably excellent crème brûlée.

Earlier, she had made her excuses for missing the rehearsal to the other guests and taken her seat, and as far as he could tell, the three not privy to the twin switch had no idea they had been fooled.

Mac would've known immediately, though, even if he hadn't been let in on the secret. During the past week, he'd gotten to know Jessie too well.

He knew the scent of her hair, her habit of placing a

protective hand on her nervous stomach and popping antacids as if they were candy. But most disturbing of all, he'd know it was her because of the way his body responded to the sound of her voice or the sight of her when she entered a room.

"I'll make it up to you for being late, Mac," Jenna whispered in his ear.

He forced a smile and nodded, too disconcerted to speak. All week he'd told himself that simply seeing Jenna again would make everything right, reconfirm his decision to marry.

But when she had arrived and rushed to his side, the expected relief never surfaced; her whisper in his ear just now had failed to stir him. And no matter how hard he tried to deny it, the thought of spending the rest of his life with Jenna left him feeling empty and trapped.

With the two sisters in the same room, he couldn't hide from the truth any longer. One look at Jessie, and his only thought was that he wanted her love and the chance to make her dreams come true.

He needed the very things he'd convinced himself he had no use for and now doubted he could live without. How could he have been so wrong about something so important?

He couldn't go through with the wedding.

The realization stunned him. Wasn't he the guy who had always prided himself on making a decision and never looking back?

Not this time. If he married Jenna, regret would eventually suck any light or joy out of his life and that wouldn't be fair to either one of them.

After the dinner he would break the news to Jenna in private.

Jessie's gaze suddenly met his, and the color drained from her face. She stood, mumbled an excuse and hurried from the room.

Had she seen the truth in his eyes?

He had to talk to her.

Removing his cell phone from his pocket, he made a show of checking the screen for a phone number as if someone had called while he'd put the phone on silent mode. "This call is important, Jenna. I'll be right back."

"Take as long as you need. I'm not going anywhere."

He left the dining room and quickly caught up with Jessie. "I need to talk to you, Jess."

"Go away, Mac," she said without turning around.

"You know. I saw it in your eyes. You know I can't go through with the wedding."

"You have to."

He pulled her into an empty alcove that housed a pay phone. "I never intended to hurt Jenna. You know that."

"Then don't."

"I don't have a choice."

"We all have choices."

He shook his head. "I had two visitors at my office last night, my mom and Craig. They confirmed what I was beginning to suspect but didn't want to admit."

"I don't want to know."

"I was determined to do the right thing for the wrong reasons, and I thought seeing Jenna again would eliminate any doubts, but it's done just the opposite. I know now that marriage without love *is* a mistake."

Jessie turned to walk away, but he gently pulled her close, cupped her face with his hands and forced her to meet his gaze. "The life I thought I wanted would be an empty one. You've shown me that, Jess. I don't have a choice about calling off the wedding because I've fallen in love with you."

"Oh, God, how did this happen?" Tears fell from her eyes. "Even if this didn't involve my sister at all, nothing can change the fact that we're wrong for each other. You don't want children and will never put family first, two things that are very important to me."

"Look, I'm not saying I can change overnight, but for the first time ever, I'm even considering the idea of being a dad, changing my priorities. But I'll need time to get used to the idea."

"It's not that simple. I could never put my own happiness over my sister's and betray Jenna in such a cruel way. Not to mention how the idea of us together would devastate my parents."

"I love you, Jessie. I can't, I won't ignore that."

"For Jenna's sake, I hope you will. Because even if you cancel the wedding, we can't be together."

"I know it will be difficult, but—"

Jessie shook her head. "Not difficult, impossible. Please don't ask me to give up my family for you, because that's the price I'd have to pay for us to be together, and I can't."

He wanted to contradict, argue, plead his case, anything and everything to keep her from walking away, but he let her go—because she was right.

Dammit, anyway. He understood loyalty, how torn Jessie felt. He even admired her for it, probably wouldn't love her as much if she were the type who could act so selfishly.

Even though patience didn't come easily to him, somehow, in the next weeks, months, maybe even years, he'd learn to live with the gaping hole in his heart, in his life, left by Jessie when she had walked away from him, from their love.

Time was his only ally now. Eventually, her parents and sister might forgive them both. The passing of time might allow Jessie to change her mind.

Regardless, he couldn't possibly marry Jenna when he'd found the love he craved in Jessie.

Chapter Nine

Jessie returned to the dining room with dread in every step. How could she face Jenna, their parents and the others and pretend nothing had changed when her world had been torn apart by the bittersweet news that Mac loved her but they could never be together?

If she knew for certain that Mac was going to cancel the wedding, she'd warn her sister, but at the moment she was helpless to do anything but continue acting the supportive maid of honor.

Dessert plates had been removed; the guests were gathering their things to leave.

She walked over to her parents to say goodbye.

"Thanks for covering for your sister, Jessie-girl," her father whispered in her ear as he hugged her.

"Everything was perfect, don't you think?" her mother asked. "And Mac's mother is a delight."

"Yes to both. But it's been a long day, so I'm going to see if Jenna is ready to go. See you tomorrow."

She apologized to the minister one last time for missing the rehearsal and accepted a brotherly hug from Craig as the two men walked out together.

"Jessie?"

She turned to find Mac's mother at her side.

"I'm sorry we didn't get a chance to talk much, but since I barely had time to say hello to Jenna at the rehearsal, I wanted to spend time getting to know her tonight."

I'm sorry for all the lies. "Think nothing of it. We'll have time to talk tomorrow." If there still *was* a wedding.

"It's amazing how much you and Jenna look alike. People must get you confused all the time."

Jessie forced a smile and clutched her stomach, the conversation skirting too close to the truth for comfort. "Not so much anymore. We're very different."

"I don't doubt that at all."

The woman with the kind eyes studied Jessie and she knew if she didn't escape quickly, she'd end up blurting out the truth. "I'd better grab Jenna. It was nice talking to you, Mrs. McKenna."

She hurried through the front door in time to notice Mac's polite smile as he said his goodbyes and was relieved to find that no one else seemed aware of anything amiss.

"Are you ready, Jenna? You've got a big day tomorrow." Jessie had already made plans to spend the night at her sister's apartment.

Jenna smiled and hugged Mac's arm. "You go on, sis.

I need some alone time with my fiancé. Mac will give me a ride home."

Jessie hesitated, but really had no choice. Mac would do what he felt he had to do. "Okay. I'll wait up," she promised, and prayed the night would end without Jenna's heart being broken.

They had shared a lot of things as twins. Broken hearts didn't need to be one of them.

"I'm glad we have a chance to be alone," Jenna said as she sat on one of several benches in the courtyard that provided the main dining room with a spectacular view. "Before the wedding tomorrow, I want to explain about *why* I left town. I want to answer all your questions in case you have any doubts."

"It's too late."

"What do you mean?"

Mac stuffed his hands in his pockets and braced himself to do the hardest thing he'd ever had to do. "I never meant to hurt you. I'm truly sorry, but I can't go through with the wedding. Not tomorrow, not ever."

"Mac." Jenna stood and put her hand on his arm. "You have every right to be upset. I admit that the reason I left town might have had something to do with me getting cold feet, but within twenty-four hours I realized I really do want to marry you. The only reason I *stayed* the extra days was because of an allergic reaction to eye cream."

"Then you're just fooling yourself. Your cold feet knew exactly what they were doing. We don't love each other, never claimed to, and deep down you knew that we were marrying for the wrong reasons. We both deserve more."

Jenna drew back, her eyes brimming with unshed tears. "*You* were the one who said that love is an unnecessary complication, an opinion I happen to share. What could've changed your view on marriage in one week?"

"Ironically enough, it was all the prewedding stuff. The surprise shower at the office, talking to the minister, things Craig and my mom mentioned yesterday."

"I have no idea what you're talking about."

"Marriage is a good thing, working together as a team for a noble cause is a good thing, but without love, it'll never be enough, never last." He had to at least try to help her understand. "Love is the glue that holds the union together, through the good times and the bad."

"You sound like a complete stranger. What's happened to you?"

"I'm calling off the wedding, but it doesn't have to affect our business partnership, unless this changes your mind about working with me."

She shook her head. "This can't be happening."

He reached for her, but she stepped away. "I have the wedding planner's phone number," he continued. "I'll call and tell her to get started on the cancellations for tomorrow. I'll absorb all the expense. You can go ahead and use the tickets to Hawaii or turn them in. I really am sorry, Jenna."

"Sorry doesn't come close to making up for the humiliation of being jilted." She stormed out of the courtyard and he followed her to the restaurant's circular driveway. She waved down a taxi and hurried inside, but held the door open. "Go to hell, Mac. And take your partnership with you."

Mac watched the taxi speed away in the direction of her apartment, where Jessie waited, ready to comfort and probably join in on calling him every bad name they could think of.

Jessie. Could a heart actually ache? His felt as if it had been pounded with a heavy gavel. He'd been a fool to think telling Jenna that he had to cancel the wedding was the hardest thing he'd ever done.

No, the most difficult challenge still lay ahead. He'd just sentenced himself to living each day with the knowledge that he might not ever have a chance with the woman he really loved.

"That dirtbag." Anger nearly burned off Jenna as she paced her kitchen floor. "That louse, that scum."

The hot tea Jessie had made remained untouched, no doubt because her sister wasn't even close to being ready to calm down.

"He doesn't even care that he's made me the laughingstock of our colleagues, my family."

Jessie hated seeing her sister suffer, felt almost sick with guilt at the thought she was responsible. But she needed to put her own feelings aside for now. She put her arm around Jenna's shoulders, still shaking with anger. "I'm sure that's not true, but either way, you wouldn't want to marry someone who wasn't sure."

"Are you kidding? A quickie divorce would be less painful than public humiliation." Jenna pulled away and continued to pace. "We had our future all planned. It was perfect. I've got to know what made everything fall apart. Tell me again what happened while I was gone."

Jessie gave a condensed version of the events of the past week, careful to omit the details of the chemistry between her and Mac and the scorching kisses shared in her backyard.

"I don't see it. Mac mentioned he'd talked with his mom and Craig yesterday. Do you have any idea what they could've said?"

"Look, Jenna, what's the point in figuring out why? This isn't about you, it's about Mac."

Jenna's eyes narrowed. "How do you know that?"

Jessie's hand clutched her churning stomach that was fed up with all the subterfuge. "You came back from Austin, glowing, ready to get married, so it has to be him."

"No, something's wrong here. You talked to him tonight, didn't you? You knew he was going to call off the wedding before I did and you didn't even warn me."

"I couldn't. There was a chance he would change his mind. I prayed that he would."

"But why would he confide in you?"

"We spent a lot of time together last week while I was filling in for you. I guess he felt he could trust me."

Jenna narrowed her eyes and glared. "Just how close did you two get while I was gone?"

Jessie felt the color drain from her face. Dear God, what was she going to do?

"You never were a good poker player, Jess." Jenna's eyes flashed with anger. "I can't believe it. My own sister has stabbed me in the back. How do you have the nerve to be here after what you've done?"

"It's not what you think. We didn't plan for this to happen."

"Why am I surprised? You've always been jealous of me. You probably couldn't stand the fact that I was getting married before you. You must've been thrilled when I handed you the perfect opportunity to steal him from me."

"It wasn't like that at all. I didn't want to stand in for you in the first place, remember? But you talked me into it. And because you refused to come back, we kept getting thrown together," Jessie added, not as an excuse for her own behavior, but to prove her sister wasn't completely blameless. "I saw he was so much more than the self-absorbed workaholic that I had imagined, but none of that matters. I made it clear to him there could never be anything between us. I wouldn't betray you like that."

Jenna stormed over to the phone and dialed. "Sorry for the late call, Mom, but I've got some bad news. Have Dad listen in."

"Jenna, what are you doing?" Jessie asked as she walked toward her.

Jenna's mouth was set in a grim line; she motioned for Jessie to stop. "Mom, Dad, I want you both to know I'll be leaving for Hawaii tomorrow, by myself, since Mac called off the wedding. And the reason it's canceled is because your daughter, the one person I thought I could trust, decided she wanted my fiancé for herself."

Jenna handed the phone to Jessie. "Try explaining it to them. Maybe they'll believe your story."

Jessie stared at the receiver in her hand.

"And after you hang up the phone, get out and don't come back. Ever."

Jenna grabbed a bottle of wine from the fridge and a glass and stalked to her bedroom, slamming the door behind her.

"Jessie, what's going on?" her mother asked. "Is it true? The wedding is canceled?"

"There has to be some mistake, right Jessie-girl?" Her father's tone sounded incredulous. "You'd never do something like that to your sister."

"It is my fault, but it's not what you think and it's too complicated to explain over the phone. I'll come by tomorrow."

"No," her mother said. "This is too horrible. I won't be able to face anyone. My God, we had most of the faculty and some of the alumni coming. And the mayor. How will I ever face those people again? How could you do this to us?"

"Jessie, your mother is too upset to talk right now."

"Then we'll talk Sunday, at dinner."

"Considering what's happened, I think it's best to cancel it. We all need some time to let this digest."

The load of guilt she'd been carrying around all week grew even heavier at the sound of disappointment in her father's voice. The dial tone thundered in her ear. That was it. No chance to explain or even ask for forgiveness.

Her tears proved almost blinding as Jessie staggered from the apartment to her car.

If only she had refused to stand in for Jenna at the final fitting for her wedding gown. Then Saturday night wouldn't have happened, either, which had led to Mac's apology on Sunday, the true beginning of her troubles.

Although the chemistry between them had existed

from the start, she could have ignored a simple case of lust. But when she'd discovered the driving force behind Mac's passion for his work, why he never wanted to have children, her heart had begun to soften and she could no longer discard him as a self-absorbed workaholic.

The more they were thrown together, the more reasons she found to love him, but she never, ever, would've acted on those feelings. Family had always come first with her and she'd never do anything that might tear them apart.

Tears fell even harder as she realized not only had she walked away from the man she loved, but also her worst nightmare had come true—she was now alienated from her family.

Mac observed the morning crowd gathered in the Marriott's restaurant. He assumed the majority were guests of the hotel. Casually dressed and smiling, he doubted they had anything more stressful planned for their Saturday than visiting friends, shopping at the upscale Willow Bend Mall or antiquing in old downtown Plano.

God, he envied them.

"Son, just spit it out. I can tell something is wrong."

"Don't you wish now that you'd gotten a hotel downtown this time? It would've been more convenient."

"I'm a creature of habit. I know where everything is in this hotel. And I'm still waiting for you to tell me what's going on."

"Shouldn't we order first?" Mac asked as he pretended to study the menu. He had asked his mother to have breakfast with him at her hotel, since telling her the bad news over the phone wasn't an option. But the words refused to come.

"Absolutely not. You only stall when it's bad news. I'll stick with the coffee I already have, at least until I hear how bad it is."

He studied the amazing woman sitting across from him. His mother had always been the perfect mix of toughness and tenderness. She was loving, yet never one to back down from a fight; direct, she always had an opinion, but kept an open mind.

"I canceled the wedding," he finally managed. "But that's not the worst of it."

She raised her eyebrows. "Which is?"

How could he tell her, without coming off as a complete jerk? What kind of man falls in love with his fiancée's sister? He leaned forward. "I didn't mean for it to happen, and I'm more surprised than anyone that it did, but I'm in love with Jessie Taggert, not Jenna."

His mother offered a sad smile and put her small hand over his. "The heart sometimes has a mind of its own. I'm proud of you for listening to yours."

Not quite the reaction he'd expected. "You don't seem surprised."

"I'm not. When I saw how you looked at the woman I thought was Jenna at the rehearsal, I was so happy for you. I knew you'd found your soul mate. But then at the dinner an hour later, there didn't seem to be that connection anymore."

"I was that obvious?"

"Only to someone who *really* knows you. When I caught you sneaking glances at Jessie when you thought no one was looking, I put two and two together and realized Jessie, for whatever reason, must've taken Jenna's place at the rehearsal."

He shook his head in amazement. "Nothing ever did get by you. What would you have done if I'd gone ahead and married Jenna tonight?"

"I would have supported your decision. It's your life, Mac. But I'm not going to lie and say I'm sorry you bit the bullet and did what was right." His mother squeezed his hand. "So, when do I get to meet my *real* future daughter-in-law?"

Mac sunk back into his chair. "I wish I knew. It wasn't until I saw Jenna again at the rehearsal dinner that I knew for sure that I couldn't go through with the wedding. When I told Jessie how I felt about her last night, she flat out told me that how we might feel about one another didn't matter." He could still see the unshed tears in her eyes, the determined set of her shoulders as she walked away.

"So that's it? You're just going to accept that?"

"For now. I've put her in the impossible position of having to choose between me and her family. And besides, I've got to work out some of my own issues first, before I pressure her."

"What is there to sort out? You love each other. Her family will come around in time."

"It's more complicated. Jessie is adamant about wanting kids and a man who puts his family first. I'm not sure if I can or even want to do either one of those things."

"But why? You'd make a wonderful father and although the work you do is important, there's more to life."

"My work is my life. You of all people should know that. Too many people lose someone they love because of inept doctors and hospitals. I want to lower those odds."

"But you don't have to sacrifice a personal life to do that. Having your own children doesn't detract from your life, they enrich it."

"Until you lose that child. Then your world crashes. I don't know how you survived Luke dying so young, but I don't ever want to take the chance of that happening to me."

Tears pooled in his mother's eyes as she squeezed his hand. "Oh, Mac. You've got it so wrong. Of course it was gut wrenching to lose a child so young, and there were times the pain was so unbearable I didn't know if I could make it through another day. But I wouldn't trade one moment I *did* have with him, just to be spared the pain of losing him later. Your brother was a precious gift and I'm grateful for the time we did have."

"But—"

She shook her head. "Being a parent isn't for everyone. And if you truly don't ever want to have children, I'll support that choice. Just remember, there are no guarantees in life, but I *can* guarantee you'll have an empty life if you let fear influence important decisions."

"Jessie and I need some time to think things through."

"Son, none of us know how much time we have on this earth. But aside from that, it's not like you to just sit back and wait. You're tenacious, that's why you're so good in that courtroom. Why aren't you willing to go to battle for something as important as the woman you love?"

"Look, even if I decided I could give Jessie what she needs to be happy, she's already made up her mind. Until enough time passes that Jenna can forgive her, and me, I risk losing Jessie for good if I push too hard now."

"Well, I hope you're right." His mother took a sip of coffee. "So what will you do, now that you won't be going on your honeymoon? Jump right back into work, I suppose?"

Mac hadn't given the immediate future any thought. Normally, work would offer the perfect distraction, but for some reason, the idea held no appeal, so maybe he was burned out after all. "No. I'll be able to think better if I get out of the city."

He recalled the interview with the minister and how Jessie had mentioned she'd always wanted to visit Hot Springs, a tourist town with springs that supposedly had the power to heal.

But could that magic water cure a broken heart? There was only one way to find out. "I'm going to drive up to Hot Springs for a few days."

Jessie continually checked the time all day Saturday. After her many naps, she noted the time on her clock radio. Never one to nap before, the depression or fatigue or both kept calling her back to bed and under the covers.

She kept track of the passing hours as she cleaned out the numerous closets in her house, a chore that usually filled her with dread. But today, the mindless task offered comfort, no doubt because her personal life was such a mess.

But the closer it got to seven, when her sister

should've been getting married, the more Jessie's attention drifted to her watch. Her stomach was beyond the help of antacids by now.

The phone rang. She let the machine record another message from Dana, the concern apparent in her voice. Carla had also called several times, obviously just as worried and puzzled over the canceled wedding and Jessie's silence.

Normally, Jessie would've turned to her friends for comfort, but she didn't deserve their sympathy. She'd ruined her sister's chance at happiness and had no one to blame but herself.

And for the millionth time she wondered how Mac was holding up. As close as he and his mother obviously were, breaking the news about the canceled wedding must've been difficult.

Jessie was certain he would turn to work for solace, probably become even more single-minded about his cause than before, even more determined to keep love out of his life.

She hated the part of her that had felt relief over the news he'd called off the wedding; she didn't even know how it was possible, since her plea for him to reconsider had been sincere. Somehow, she would have found a way to embrace his marriage to her sister; she would have wished them well, then gone off to live her own life, find some happiness of her own.

Her eyes filled with tears yet again, but this time she simply let them fall freely; she had helped to create the hopeless situation and there wasn't a damn thing she could do about it.

The doorbell rang, interrupting her self-pity party. Jessie contemplated hiding out in the closet, but suspected her visitor, either Dana or Carla, would consider the situation an emergency and barge in.

Taking a deep breath, Jessie stepped around the clutter on the closet floor to find some tissue. On the way to the front door she wiped her eyes, blew her nose, then peeked through the curtain to check the identity of her visitor.

Both friends stood on her porch, their expressions determined. Jessie groaned.

"We know you're in there, Jess."

"We're not leaving until you talk to us. We're warning you, we both have keys and aren't afraid to use them."

She reluctantly opened the door.

"Thank God you're okay, Jess." Carla hugged her then held Jessie at arm's length. "Why aren't you answering your phone?"

"Now that I know you're okay, I want to strangle you, girl," Dana said, and moved in for a hug of her own. "The message you left just said the wedding was canceled. No details. Then the wedding planner called later with the same message. What happened?"

"It's all my fault. Jenna and my parents are never going to speak to me again. And Mac, Mac…" Tears fell and she couldn't speak, couldn't bear to say out loud that she'd never be with the man she loved.

Carla eased Jessie onto the sofa. "Dana, why don't you make some hot tea. I think our girl could use it."

"Good idea." Dana left for the kitchen while Carla fetched a box of tissues from the nearest bathroom.

Minutes later, Dana returned with a tray loaded with three cups of steaming tea, spoons and sugar, then took a seat on the other side of Jessie.

Jessie inhaled the cinnamon-honey aroma and already felt calmer. She took a sip. The warm liquid soothed her throat, raw from all the crying the past twenty-four hours. "Thanks. I guess I did need this."

"You're welcome." Carla leaned forward. "Now, tell us what happened. How can any of this be your fault?"

Tears fell and Jessie reached for another tissue to wipe them away. "It's hard to explain because I don't understand it myself. All I do know is that Mac and I somehow fell in love in less than a week and I hate myself for allowing it to happen."

Jessie stared straight ahead, unable to look her friends in the eye.

Silence.

"I know you're shocked, believe me, so am I, but it's the awful truth. I honestly tried to talk Mac into going through with the wedding, I even told him that we couldn't ever be together no matter what happened, but he called it off anyway."

"Of course he did," Carla replied. "And he did the right thing." She put her hand on Jessie's closest arm. "Jessie, hon, I saw how that man looked at you when you were kissing in your backyard, and you, you were as lost in that kiss as he was. The man had no choice."

"But we both knew it was wrong. We should have fought it more."

"You can't always dictate whether or not you're

going to love someone, Jess," Carla insisted. "Sometimes it just happens."

Dana reached for Jessie's other arm. "I didn't see the kiss, but it sounds like there was just too much chemistry to ignore. And if you toss love in with the chemistry, no one can fight that combination."

Jessie shook her head. "When we first met, Mac told me that he wasn't looking for love or chemistry, just a partner, and Jenna was the perfect choice because she felt the same way. Then he and I are thrown together and from day one there was incredible chemistry between us. What are the odds?"

"Wait a minute," Carla said. "No love, no chemistry? What the heck were they getting married for?"

"It's complicated." Jessie briefly filled her friends in on Mac's past, how the loss of his brother had affected decisions about his professional and personal life. "But Mac obviously wanted the marriage as much as Jenna did, since he agreed with me two days ago that what happened in my backyard was a mistake and could never happen again."

"But then twenty-four hours later he changes his mind?" Dana piped in.

Jessie nodded. "He thought seeing Jenna again would take away any doubt, but it did the opposite." Jessie revealed how he'd followed her out of the dining room at the rehearsal dinner and told her that he loved her and couldn't go through with the wedding. "I could never put my happiness over Jenna's. I told him that he should go ahead and marry her, because he and I could never be together. It would tear my family apart, and I would never risk that."

"But, Jess," Dana said. "He shouldn't marry Jenna if he doesn't love her. That wouldn't be fair to either of them."

Jessie shook her head. "That's just it. They never *were* in love, and that's how they both wanted it. Until I came along."

"It's clear Jenna wasn't ready to marry," Carla argued. "If she had been, she would never have run off with her ex-boyfriend a week before her wedding."

"Right," Dana added. "It's obvious the marriage wasn't meant to be. She and Mac were marrying for the wrong reasons."

"Why they wanted to marry isn't the issue," Jessie insisted. "I didn't mean to, but I *did* steal her fiancé. Sisters don't do that to each other. But I swear, I never meant to fall in love with him. I fought it. We both did."

Carla covered Jessie's closest hand with her own. "Anyone who knows you knows you wouldn't purposely hurt anyone, and especially not Jenna."

"And if your family can't understand that and cares so little about your happiness, Jess," Dana said, "then maybe you should focus on you and Mac and *your* future. The two of you can create your own family."

"That's exactly why the idea of a future with Mac is ridiculous. All of this is for nothing. Mac told me last night that his mind isn't as closed to the possibility of changing his priorities, of having children, but what if he really doesn't want to change, and is only saying that because he doesn't want to lose me?"

"Jessie, hon, there isn't any way you can know for sure. Only time will tell."

"Yeah, shouldn't you at least give him a chance to prove himself?"

Jessie shook her head. "That's not the only thing. He's too controlling. Once he got a whiff of the idea I had an interest in being a principal, he tried to steam-roll me into switching careers. I want the man I love to be satisfied with who I am."

"But, Jess," Carla piped in. "*You're* not satisfied. He probably just wants you to be happy and is trying to help."

"If and when I change careers, it has to be *my* decision. And all of this is beside the point. In time, my family will have to forgive me, but that won't ever happen if I give in to my feelings for Mac."

"Listen to what you're saying, Jess," Dana insisted. "Are you really going to choose your family, who isn't concerned about what you want or need right now, over the man you love and who says he loves you?"

Jessie moaned and put her head in her hands. "Before I met Mac, I thought I knew what I was doing. What happened to my neat, orderly life?"

Carla patted Jessie's head. "Honey, love happened. The question is, what are you going to do about it?"

Jessie wished she knew.

Chapter Ten

Jessie watched the early morning antics of the birds as she thumbed through the sales ads of the thick Sunday paper, but knew that what she was really looking for—understanding from her parents and forgiveness from Jenna—couldn't be found between those glossy pages.

The first couldn't happen until she'd resolved things with her sister, but how?

The squawking grew louder and she glanced up to discover two birds fighting over the last bit of birdseed in one of the feeders. Maybe they were sisters, Jessie thought sadly, although in all honesty, she and her sister hadn't fought until now.

Jessie had always been the one to give in, whether it was a tennis match or agreeing to do a favor. She even suspected a small part of why she hadn't pursued the idea of becoming a principal was because she didn't want to be seen as competing with Jenna, who agreed with their parents that teaching wasn't prestigious enough for a Taggert.

So what had changed? Why was she now ready to risk a new career? Had she suddenly morphed into a super-competitive person who wasn't afraid to tackle a new job, a person without a conscience who didn't care who she hurt and had chased after Mac out of jealousy?

No. Jessie knew in her heart that she wasn't in competition with her sister in any way. She and Mac had even fought their feelings, but the emotional connection had proven too strong to ignore.

The birds continued to squabble and she shook her head over their stubbornness, which reminded her of Mac. He was the most tenacious, determined man she'd ever met. He had even bragged about never looking back once he'd made a choice.

And yet, concerning one of the biggest decisions of his life—marriage—he'd listened to his heart and done what must have been incredibly difficult, calling off the wedding at the last minute.

The man had guts. The man had faith in her, loved her. *Mac* had acted as the catalyst for the changes in her life, had helped her to grow and change.

And now that love had happened, what was she going to do about it?

Suddenly, she knew the answer to that question, which had been posed by her friend the night before. Jessie was through with making decisions based on what other people thought; she no longer believed in doing the wrong thing for the right reason.

She'd squawk and squabble, do whatever it took to win the man she loved.

She reached for the phone and called Jenna's hotel in Hawaii, but had no luck reaching her. Even though she doubted it would do any good, Jessie left a message for her sister to call.

Too much had built up inside to wait for Jenna's return, so Jessie grabbed a yellow tablet of paper and poured her heart out onto the lined sheets. She admitted she loved Mac and closed with the hope that in time Jenna and their parents would forgive her, realize she never intended to hurt anyone, and understand why she had to follow her heart.

She addressed and stamped the envelope, then put it in her purse to mail in the morning.

Next, Jessie needed to locate Mac, convince him to give them another chance. She called his home, office and cell phone, but only connected with his voice mail.

His secretary had to know where he was. Jessie dialed information for Taryn's number and let out a sigh of relief when she answered.

"Taryn, this is Jessie Taggert."

"Oh, hi. You're Jenna's sister, right? Isn't it awful about the wedding?"

"Taryn, I need to reach Mac. Can you tell me where he is?"

"Is it some kind of emergency? Because he made it clear he wasn't to be bothered unless it was."

Jessie was through with pretending and deception. "It's not quite an emergency, but it is very important."

"Well, I guess it's okay then. Mac is in Hot Springs at the Arlington Resort."

Taryn gave Jessie the phone number. "The canceled wedding must have upset him more than he admits, though. He told me to go through his calendar and re-schedule all his after five and weekend appointments for during office hours. How weird is that?"

A smile spread across Jessie's face and her heart felt lighter than it had in days. Mac really had been serious about changing his priorities. "Thanks, Taryn."

Jessie rushed into her bedroom to pack a suitcase. She'd mail the letter to her sister on the way to I-30, the most direct route to Arkansas.

Mac tossed his clothes into his suitcase. The trip to Hot Springs had been a mistake. Everywhere he went he spotted couples and families, which only reminded him of what he didn't have and only recently even knew he wanted.

Earlier that morning he had escaped into the darkness of the visitor center to watch the film that retold the history of the town, which had grown into a bustling tourist attraction with amazing speed once news spread of the healing abilities of the water.

The short movie had left him with heavy thoughts about faith, change and time. People had come to Hot Springs from all over the country believing they would find relief if not a cure. The town changed and benefited because of that faith. But the surge of prosperity couldn't last forever, and in time, the spas and elegant hotels had been abandoned. Many years later, tourism had once again made Hot Springs a popular destination.

He needed to have faith in his love for Jessie, trust that the joys of fatherhood would far outweigh any possible pain. Life could change in an instant and he shouldn't take time for granted.

His mother had tried to tell him all of that earlier, but he'd been too stubborn to listen. But he should have. Hundreds of miles away, he didn't stand a chance of convincing Jessie they had a future. Once he was back in town he would find her and—

"Skipping town, Counselor?"

He turned at the sound of the familiar voice that never failed to capture his full attention. Had he dreamed up the angel in the doorway dressed in a navy-and-white sundress and looking more beautiful than he remembered?

He quickly closed the distance between them and gently gripped her shoulders to prove that she wasn't a hallucination. "I might as well. I came here looking for a cure, but I never could find any of the magical water someone told me about. Unless it just doesn't work on broken hearts."

"Maybe there's something I can do to help." She cupped his face with her hands and ran her thumbs across his lips, her gentle touch pure torture.

He pulled her tightly against him and breathed in her scent, marveled at how right she felt in his arms. "I'm feeling better already," he whispered, barely able to speak, his throat tight with emotion.

"I was wrong to turn you away, Mac. Tell me it's not too late to give us a chance."

"I was going to cut out of here early because all I could think about was you," he offered between hungry kisses. "I had planned to spend the next few days building a strong case for why we belong together. Then, I'd be tenacious and persuasive, just like in the courtroom, and hound you until you couldn't say no."

She tilted her head back, her mouth curved in a smile. "Is that right?"

"Definitely. Because if you haven't figured it out yet, when I want something, I go after it, and I want you. You've shown me that love and family are what really matters in life. I love you, Jessie. Will you marry me?"

"Yes," she replied, her green eyes dancing with excitement. "But not because of your power of persuasion." Her expression turned tender. "What won me over is your big heart and willingness to open that heart and let me in. I hope my family will someday bless our marriage, but until then, *we'll* be family."

"No objection from me, but we'd better start looking right away for that perfect house with the big backyard. What were you thinking, two kids, three?"

She grinned. "Two, for sure. And a dog. We can negotiate the rest later. Meanwhile, is it too late to let the front desk know you've changed your mind about checking out?"

"It's never too late."

"Good, because there's a Jacuzzi we need to visit later on, when no one is around. We can put the jets on high and make lots of bubbles…"

God, he loved this woman. He gazed into her sparkling eyes and knew with certainty, the way he sometimes knew the jury's vote before he was told, that he and Jessie belonged together.

Epilogue

Six months later

Jessie rang the doorbell. Within seconds, the door opened and Henri wrapped her in their traditional hug.

"Ms. Jessie!" He held her at arm's length to look at her. "It's been much too long since I see that beautiful smile. But I can tell that you're happy, yes?"

She smiled. "Very." She motioned to Mac. "Henri, you remember Mac McKenna. Did Mother tell you about…us?"

"But of course. No secrets in this house. Congratulations." Henri hugged Mac. Then the chef's expression turned somber. "You make my Jessie happy, and we have no problems."

Mac put his arm across her shoulders. "I'm going to do my best, sir."

Jessie's skin tingled from his touch even after six months together; she suspected he'd always have that effect on her.

Henri nodded. "Good. I prepared a special dessert in honor of your marriage. I'm just sad I could not do your wedding cake. It would have been *magnifique*."

"I'm sure tonight's treat will be just as wonderful." Jessie had to admit, though, that she would've preferred a more traditional wedding and reception, but considering the circumstances and the fact that she and Mac didn't want to wait to marry, eloping to Vegas had made a lot more sense.

She had absolutely no regrets. Mac supported her, challenged her, loved her.

"And don't worry, my Jessie. Jenna will come around. She's lost without you. Just give her time." Henri drew her in for another hug. "And when she hears about your little one," he whispered, "your sister won't be able to stay away."

Jessie gasped. She wasn't showing yet, it was too early in her pregnancy. "But how did you know?"

He grinned. "I'm French. We know these things. Now, go inside. Your parents are waiting just inside the door."

"But they never—"

"This has been very hard on them, too, Jessie. Now, go," he said as he shooed them toward the door. "Tell them your good news. There's nothing like a baby to bring a family together again."

"Do you think your parents already know, too?" Mac whispered in Jessie's ear.

She chuckled. "No way. Not a drop of French blood between them."

Jessie opened the door. The mouthwatering aroma of baked salmon and rice barely registered in her brain because of the startling sight of her parents holding hands in the foyer, their expressions uncertain.

Jessie hated the awkwardness, wanted the healing to begin. She smiled. "Hello, Grandma and Grandpa."

Her mother's eyes grew wide. "What?"

"You mean—"

Jessie nodded. "I'm due in September!"

Both parents rushed to her side and took turns hugging her, then showered Mac with the same treatment.

Tears filled her mother's eyes as she reached for both of Jessie's hands. "This is wonderful news. Can you forgive us for not being there for you these past months? We had to stand by your sister, Jessie. You had Mac, and she had no one."

"We all did what we had to do." Too much time had already been spent cut out of each other's lives. Jessie's heart was too full of happiness and hope to play the blame game. "The important thing is we're trying to be a family again."

"And it will happen, Jess," her dad promised. "Jenna is back on her feet again. She's moved to Ft. Worth and has a job with the most prestigious firm in town, so at least her professional life is back on track. Just give her some time. She'll come around."

"Of course she will, Dad. We're not just sisters, we're twins. And once she hears our news, I know she won't be able to stay away."

"This calls for a toast. Henri," her father called out. "Do we have any champagne?" He put his arm around Mac and began to walk toward the dining room. "Son, your life is about to change drastically."

"I'm counting on it, sir."

Her mother put an arm around Jessie's waist as they followed the men into the dining room. As usual, the table looked exquisite.

"So, are you going to continue to teach until you have the baby?"

Jessie had assumed the subject of her career would come up, but she had enough confidence now that she could simply give the facts and not worry about being judged. "Yes, and I had already begun classes to get my mid-management certificate, but now that I'm pregnant, I'm not sure what to do."

"I can certainly understand that. The job of principal requires *more* time than a teacher, not less, and with a newborn, it might not be the best time to switch careers."

Jessie blinked. "But you were always so set on me moving up."

Her mother sighed. "I know. But I've had a lot of time to think these past few months, and I realize we're different people. I probably shouldn't have tried to press my views and goals onto you."

"Probably?"

"Don't push it," her mother teased. "It's the closest thing to an apology you're going to get."

Jessie laughed. "I accept."

Henri was busy pouring champagne into four glasses and sparkling water into the fifth.

"I can't believe I'm going to be a grandma. You must let me get Yvonne to decorate your nursery. She did this wonderful fairy theme for Deedee's grand-daughter's room, but of course you'll want something different."

Jessie chuckled and shook her head. Some things never changed. "We'll see. We're focusing more on names right now."

"Is it too late to add one more plate?"

"Ms. Jenn!" Henri said, beaming. "I get another glass!"

Jessie turned around to find her sister rushing toward her. "Can you forgive me for the hateful things I said? For being so selfish and expecting you to walk away from real love just to spare me embarrassment?"

"Of course." Jessie hugged her sister tight. "As long as you forgive me for causing you the embarrassment and pain to begin with."

"Done." Jenna leaned back until she faced Jessie. "It's been horrible not having you to talk to, but it's made me realize that I've never stopped seeing you as competition, which is crazy. I don't want anything to ever come between us again."

"I couldn't agree more," Jessie said, blinking back tears of joy.

"Good. Because I'm warning you now, I'm going to want to spend lots of time with my niece or nephew."

Jessie laughed, not even a little surprised that her twin already knew. "We're going to hold you to that."

Jenna hugged Jessie one more time then approached Mac and kissed him on the cheek. "Congratulations,

Mac. I'm happy for you and Jessie. Honest. And I know you'll be a great dad."

"Thanks. Believe me, I'm more surprised than anyone that I fell so hard and fast, but it feels right. Better than right. And you'll find the right someone, too."

Jenna rolled her eyes. "There's as much of a chance of me becoming a blushing bride and mother as the Cowboys winning another Super Bowl any time soon. No offense, Dad."

"Well, I do take offense. We had a good draft. It could happen, you mark my word."

Laughter filled the room. Jessie might not have a typical family, but they were hers. The healing had begun.

Mac drew Jessie close. "Unlike the unpredictable Cowboys," he whispered, "there's no doubt in my mind that we're going to have a happy ending, Jess. You opened my eyes to what I really want and need to be happy. You. A family. Balance in my life."

He placed his hand against her still flat stomach. "You've filled my life with more love than I ever thought possible. I can't believe I once thought I never wanted to be a dad and now I'm counting down the days until our child is born."

"I'm excited, too, but I also intend to enjoy every stage of my pregnancy."

"And after the baby is born, we'll get to start all those traditions you're so crazy about."

True, but some things couldn't wait. "You're right, but there's one tradition we need to start right away."

His expression turned puzzled.

"Since I have this terrible sweet tooth," she whispered in his ear, "I think Sundays should involve two desserts. One after the meal with my parents, and one at home, since I can't seem to get enough of *you.*"

"Count on it," he murmured, then sealed the promise with a hungry kiss that left her craving more. "Count on me, Jess. Count on us."

"You give one heck of a closing argument, Counselor."

She certainly had no objections, no doubts they would live happily ever after.

Case closed.

* * * * *

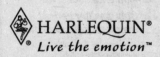

If you enjoyed what you just read,
then we've got an offer you can't resist!

Take 2 bestselling
love stories FREE!

Plus get a FREE surprise gift!

Clip this page and mail it to Silhouette Reader Service™

IN U.S.A.	IN CANADA
3010 Walden Ave.	P.O. Box 609
P.O. Box 1867	Fort Erie, Ontario
Buffalo, N.Y. 14240-1867	L2A 5X3

YES! Please send me 2 free Silhouette Romance® novels and my free surprise gift. After receiving them, if I don't wish to receive anymore, I can return the shipping statement marked cancel. If I don't cancel, I will receive 4 brand-new novels every month, before they're available in stores! In the U.S.A., bill me at the bargain price of $3.57 plus 25¢ shipping and handling per book and applicable sales tax, if any*. In Canada, bill me at the bargain price of $4.05 plus 25¢ shipping and handling per book and applicable taxes**. That's the complete price and a savings of at least 10% off the cover prices—what a great deal! I understand that accepting the 2 free books and gift places me under no obligation ever to buy any books. I can always return a shipment and cancel at any time. Even if I never buy another book from Silhouette, the 2 free books and gift are mine to keep forever.

210 SDN DZ7L
310 SDN DZ7M

Name	(PLEASE PRINT)	
Address	Apt.#	
City	State/Prov.	Zip/Postal Code

Not valid to current Silhouette Romance® subscribers.

Want to try two free books from another series?
Call 1-800-873-8635 or visit www.morefreebooks.com.

* Terms and prices subject to change without notice. Sales tax applicable in N.Y.
** Canadian residents will be charged applicable provincial taxes and GST.
All orders subject to approval. Offer limited to one per household.
® are registered trademarks owned and used by the trademark owner and or its licensee.

SROM04R

©2004 Harlequin Enterprises Limited

Do you like stories that get *up close* and *personal*?
Do you long to be loved *truly, madly, deeply...*?

If you're looking for emotionally intense, tantalizingly
tender love stories, stop searching and start reading

Harlequin Romance®

You'll find authors who'll leave you breathless, including:

Liz Fielding

Winner of the 2001 RITA Award for
Best Traditional Romance
(*The Best Man and the Bridesmaid*)

Day Leclaire

USA Today bestselling author

Leigh Michaels

Bestselling author with 30 million
copies of her books sold worldwide

Renee Roszel

USA Today bestselling author

Margaret Way

Australian star with 80 novels to her credit

Sophie Weston

A fresh British voice and a hot talent!

Don't miss their latest novels, coming soon!

HARLEQUIN®
Makes any time special®

COMING NEXT MONTH

#1754 NIGHTTIME SWEETHEARTS—Cara Colter
In a Fairy Tale World...
She never forgot the brooding bad boy who had, once upon a time, made her heart race. So when Cynthia Fosythe hears a husky, familiar voice calling to her out of the tropical moonlit night she's stunned. She'd let go of Rick Barnett to preserve her good-girl image, but now Cynthia's prepared to lay it all on the line for another chance at paradise.

#1755 INSTANT MARRIAGE, JUST ADD GROOM—
Myrna Mackenzie
Nortorious bachelor Caleb Fremont is just what baby-hungry Victoria Holbrook is looking for—the perfect candidate for the father of her child. Although Caleb isn't interested in being a dad, he's agreed to a temporary marriage of convenience. But when the stick finally turns pink will he be able to let Victoria—and his baby—go?

#1756 DADDY, HE WROTE—Jill Limber
Reclusive author Ian Miller purchased an historic farmhouse to get some much-needed peace and quiet—and overcome his writer's block. Yet when he finds that the farm comes complete with beautiful caretaker Trish Ryan and her delightful daughter, Ian might find that inspiration can be found in the most unlikely places....

#1757 KISSED BY CAT—Shirley Jump
Soulmates
When Garrett McCallister discovers a purr-fectly gorgeous woman in his veterinary clinic, wearing nothing but a lab coat, he's confused, suspicious...and very imtrigued. Will Garrett run when he discovers Catherine Wyndham's secret curse, or will he let the mysterious siren into his heart?

SRCNM0105